This is a light novel (or novella) that was originally published online as a Supernatural AU fanfiction by TheAuthorGod on Archive of Our Own (and is still available there as fanfiction, unedited, for free). Slight modifications have been made to ensure this is separated from the world of Supernatural and suitable for publishing.

ALSO

This light novel is printed using OpenDyslexic, an OpenSource font provided by opendyslexia.org that's made to help with readability. Please support their effort.

Extended Family

By Morven Moeller

Dreampunk Press

Extended Family

For more information go to dreampunkpress.com.

Summary: "In a world where children lose their ability to see colors until they meet their soulmate, Luke must find out what it means when his only slightly come back when he meets his newest next door neighbor. In the process, he finds answers, questions, and a family he'd never dreamed of."

ISBN 978-1-938215-18-6

Categories: LGBT—Fiction, SAGA—Fiction, Gay—Fiction, Lesbian—Fiction, Soulmates—Fiction, Schools—Fiction, High Schools—Fiction, Friendship—Fiction

Page Count: 124

Word Count: ~23,000

~ For graysexuals, demisexuals, and the rest of the asexual community, because there is more than one way to love.

Chapter 1:

Home is Just a Place

Despite the fact that he'd moved all of his belongings into
the nooks and crannies of the new place, Luke's room was
still bare. Some people would say that it didn't seem
homey. And Luke tended to agree, but they'd never been
in one place long enough for him to acquire a sense of
home. How would he know what a home should feel like
after living in place after place after place?

After his father died, they'd moved around a lot, never
staying in one place more than a year. There was one
place, somewhere in Ohio, that they only stayed for two
months. He was the new kid twice that school year. Of
course, he was always the new kid.

Matt pushed through Luke's door. "Hey, you done?" His mop of hair was way too long. If it had been up to Luke, Matt's hair would be buzzed. He wasn't entirely sure why Matt endured the teasing and kept his long hair. Probably had something to do with the fact that Mom called it his 'handsome mane'.

Shrugging, Luke folded down the last box and threw it on the pile he'd tuck into his closet, ready and there for when they no doubt would move again. Hell, he was almost 18. Maybe the next time he moved, he'd be going by himself. "Yeah, I guess. You got your stuff in your room?"

Ignoring his question, Matt walked over to Luke's bed and flopped backward onto it. "I feel good about this move."

"Yeah?"

"Mmm-hmm. Maybe this is the town where I'll finally meet her?" His pupils practically turned to hearts.

Luke rolled his eyes. "You say that about every move." He shut his closet door and spun to glare at his brother.

Ever since Matt lost his colors at 4, all he'd cared about was finding them again. He'd cried for weeks, making himself sick with snot and dehydration. It had been ugly. Luke remembered losing his colors, but he didn't think he was as sad about it as his brother had been. But, he'd lost his colors at the same time he had lost his Dad; it sort of just rolled into one horrible thing, becoming a 'big kid' all at once.

Crossing his arms across his chest, Matt harrumphed. "Yeah, but I especially feel it this time. And..." he dragged it out, sitting up and grinning wide, "I'm starting high school, so even more kids to meet, to see, to talk to."

"Matt, why aren't you in your room? You haven't finished unpacking yet!" Mom's voice came through the door; actually, it was so loud that it came through the walls too.

Luke chuckled while Matt hopped up and ran from the room, fear etched into his features. There was nothing scarier than Mom when she was mad.

School didn't start for a few more weeks, so Luke planned to spend the time surfing the internet. However, his mother, for all the accomplishments she'd managed to see through being a widow and single mother, still had some 'hot mess' moments.

They didn't have internet yet.

He trod down the stairs, quiet enough not to disturb his brother's reprimanding. Not wanting to point out that she'd forgotten it, Luke checked the messages and made in the call to the best internet provider in the area. They wouldn't be more expensive than the last place, but it would be a few days before they would send a guy out, overbooked or something.

Despite that he knew he had to walk up to the Starbucks for wifi, periodically Luke would open up his phone and try to check his email. They had data, but it wasn't the unlimited plan. He and Matt's phones dipped into the same data pool and Matt had a horrible sense of direction. Luke wasn't sure if Matt knew it, but he turned data off on his own phone to make sure that Matt had as much as possible.

Flopping onto the sofa and looking at his phone, Luke had to laugh. There were 5 locked wifis and 3 of them were named in a way that blamed someone called Jordan for 'breaking' them.

He looked around for the newspaper, but it wasn't on the coffee table or end table, which meant it was still out on the front step. He growled low in his throat at the ceiling before getting up to fetch it.

"Fuck you, Jordan!"

Next door, a blond kid maybe Luke's age, maybe older, ran from the house to the car. "It's not my fault that you can't put your shit away."

"You're not fucking lactose intolerant!" Another guy, this one with dark hair and a scowl, came through the door waving a menacing hand at who Luke would guess was Jordan.

The shiny sports car revved up and backed out of the drive way. Jordan rolled down the window and waved.

Luke caught sight of a shit-eating grin through the window.

"Buy more almond milk while you're at it!" The dark-haired guy flipped the driver off before pivoting to go back inside. "How am I going to have cereal before work? Fuck."

"Do you like cashew milk?" Luke piped up. His mother had issues with milk during her period, which yes, Luke knew about. He was the one that needed the explanation as to why they needed two milks and he seemed to piss his mother off just enough to get her to give him the real reasoning. Matt seemed to like the cashew milk, too.

The guy turned.

And suddenly, things looked different. Luke couldn't figure it out at first, but slowly it dawned on him.

Colors.

The grass was green and the sky was blue and the shutters were deep red. But, at the same time, everything looked kind of muted. Okay, really muted. He thought back to what the ocean looked like when he was little. He just...

The colors weren't amazing enough for him to be surprised. It was dull. It didn't make sense.

"It's not my favorite. Are you lactose intolerant, too?" The guy was frozen on his porch. He didn't act like he could suddenly see colors.

For that reason and because the colors were still muted, Luke didn't say anything. Maybe it was a lapse of judgment. Maybe he was just crazy. He didn't want to do anything weird, so he just shook his head. "Nah, my mom prefers the stuff. You want some?"

"Yeah."

The guy was pretty forward. After the spectacle with Jordan, Luke had expected him to be high-strung, like Matt. But the guy was muted, like he didn't care one way or another. That meant that Jordan-guy must have really pissed him off. Luke thought it was kind of funny, so he cracked a smile. "Come on. I'll get it." He waved the guy

6

over and turned back into the house, leaving the door open behind him.

"So, I take it all of those wifis come from your house? How did he manage to screw them all up?"

The guy followed, also leaving the door open. Luke couldn't blame him; it was probably weird following a strange guy into the next house over. Of course, Luke felt like he knew him, like they were connected now. Luke had his colors – or at least some of his colors? – because of this guy.

He didn't even know his name.

"Yeah. My brother is an ass. He messed up the password on one. He managed to overheat the router on another. And the last one stopped working with no explanation, but we all know it was probably him. I can't wait for him to leave for college next week." Having followed Luke to the kitchen, he looked around at the boxes that were still in the room. "Welcome to the neighborhood, I guess." He leaned on the counter.

Opening the fridge and pushing the half-gallon of regular milk to the side, Luke grabbed the cashew milk. He could see the color in the carrots and the broccoli, and it was definitely a myth that the color made them look more

7

appetizing. That had been one of his mother's favorite ways to get him to eat vegetables, but they still looked gross as somewhat-colored vegetables. "There should be enough for a bowl of cereal. You can just have it." He handed it over.

"Thanks." The guy turned and started toward the door.

Huffing, Luke moved to follow. "Wait, I don't know your name."

"What? That the payment for the cashew milk?"

"Actually, if we're talking payment, I'd much prefer access to your wifi. We don't have any yet."

It was an awkward moment. "Yeah, okay."

Luke looked around, kind of embarrassed since it had half-way been a joke. Where he looked, other things had that light wash of color, too. It was really underwhelming. "I was sort of joking..."

The guy tucked the carton under his arm and held out his hand. "Phone?"

"Yeah, okay this is happening." Luke pulled his phone from his pajama pants pocket and unlocked it. He handed it over. He just prayed that he didn't open safari or his tinder or something that would embarrass him even further. Honestly, he didn't know this guy; why was he turning over his phone?

Well, the world didn't end.

The un-named neighbor returned Luke's phone and continued to the door. Luke followed behind him feeling like that dog that followed Matt around for two weeks back in Illinois. He kind of just wanted to follow... dammit. "If you don't tell me your name, I'm gonna have to assign one to you. And I'm really bad at naming." Luke just wanted to keep talking. Is this how color matches worked? Obviously not, otherwise he'd have all of his colors. Is this how soulmates worked? Well, his colors were already broken so probably no.

The guy was off of the front porch and halfway across the lawn back to his house.

Luke felt the urge to keep talking. "And, I mean baaaaad at naming. Like the kind of bad that means that, when I have kids, I'll end up naming them after rock bands and bass guitarists or my partner is gonna have to name them or-"

It was strange. The guy turned around again, and, when their eyes met that time, Luke's colors became a tiny bit brighter.

"You're gay?"

"Well, I'm bi. But don't try to change the subject. I'm trying to say that I'll call you something dumb like 'Cashew' if you don't tell me a better name." Luke blushed little bit. The amount of red that tinged his face was still more than the amount of red that tinged the shutters and stripes of the flags hung on some of the houses.

The guy shrugged, "Cashew's fine." With that, he turned and took the cashew milk into his house.

Luke was thoroughly confused.

With wifi on his phone, Luke did some research into colors. First, he ended up googling how to turn off the colors on his phone. The strange shade of colors he was experiencing was annoying and the less he had to deal with it the better. There was a way to do it under accessibility and it was easy enough to switch off. He also added in a shortcut so that he could switch back and forth in the future.

10

Wikipedia had too much information on the subject. He'd ended up hopping from one highlighted link to another until he settled on "Staged Color Progression".

Staged Color Progression was a rare way to gain your colors back. Science couldn't explain it and psycolorgists had to deal with it on a Case-by-Case basis. Luke didn't have the money to see a psycolorgist or counselor, so, from his limited research, he decided to start by trying to be Cashew's friend.

Cashew, what a dumb thing to call someone.

The thought reverberated through his head all day. Through checking his email, through running errands. He couldn't get Cashew out of his head, the guy or the dumb name he'd assigned him.

"Hey, Cashew!" Luke stepped out of the car and waved at their neighbor. Cashew was sitting on the steps in front of his house. He raised a single hand in reply, not really a wave.

Matt scurried around the car and made a pointed look between the two. "Cashew?" He wrinkled his nose.

Rolling his eyes, Luke shut the door to the ambassador and pushed Matt toward the house. Despite that Matt was shorter than him now, Luke knew that one day he'd be taller than him. The kid kept having growth spurts and was already to Luke's ears despite Luke having 4 years on him. "Don't you have school supplies to organize, nerd?"

Jerking up his shoulders and making a bitchface, Matt screwed up his nose. With that, Matt turned, stomping into the house to play with his new highlighters and pencils.

Luke crossed the lawn and stopped in front of Cashew. "So, how are you, now?"

Cashew looked up and, though his face was neutral, Luke could tell somewhere in his gut that he was happy. "Pretty good, actually."

Luke's colors took another saturation growth spurt. He could see that Cashew's eyes were going to be some sort of blue at the end of all of this. Part of him couldn't wait. Why couldn't he just get all of his colors at once? What was wrong with him? Why was he broken? "Yeah? What happened? That brother of yours get put in his place?" Luke chuckled for good measure. Did he know this guy well enough to make a joke like that? No, but he felt like he did. They were becoming soulmates or something, right? Isn't that what the color thing meant?

Shifting, Cashew tilted his head. His sharp features caught the sunlight and Luke couldn't believe how angelic the guy looked. His skin was darker than Luke's, but it seemed to glow like clouds at sunset. Luke could even make out the beginning of a 5 o'clock shadow. This guy was already attractive and Luke could imagine all the ways he would fill out. How he would look once he grew into his somewhat lanky arms.

Luke's mouth watered.

These were not the kind of thoughts he had expected to have when he walked over. Wikipedia had said something about people who experience Staged Color Progression tending to take more time to fall in love with their soulmate, that they would take longer to get hit with the mushy, chick-flick crap.

Yet, here Luke was, comparing Cashew to a sunset and dreaming about a future with him. Maybe he was really broken?

"You okay there?" Cashew's hand came up to his shoulder. His fingertips seemed to burn Luke where they pressed to his shoulder through his shirts.

Luke's colors blinked further into existence. They still weren't anything like how he remembered them for childhood; part of him wondered how long it would take. Would he ever have all of his colors? "Yeah," he shook off Cashew's hand, "I'm good."

Chapter 2:

Grey-Color Alliance (GCA)

He hadn't really taken the whole thing seriously. Sometimes, people write their names and emails on club sign-up lists just for the heck of it. Maybe so that they could walk away from the table or because they want to get their brother off their back about making friends and such.

Luke had put his contact info on 3 sign-up sheets on teacher night at the beginning of the year: Men's Field Hockey Team, Robotics and Engineering Team, and the Grey-Color Alliance. He'd only really meant the one that he'd put on the Robotics and Engineering Team.

In fact, he was about to block the emails from the other clubs when something caught his eye. The president – at least, that's what Luke guessed since they were in charge of emailing new recruits — was Bella Myer, aka his neighbor.

And yeah, he'd been curious, so he had opened the email.

The second email in the list of recipients was the one and only Casper Myer, and, at that point, Luke was basically hooked. He put the information for the first meeting into his phone and set 3 different reminders.

So, those were the (un)fortunate events that brought Luke to the GCA's door. It was an English classroom on the English Department hallway and in the door's window were colorful letters "GCA".

Stealing himself, he pushed the door open and entered.

There was free food. Luke tried not to realize just how pathetic he was based on the fact that he was there more to spy on Casper than for the refreshments.

"Okay, everyone. Newbies in those chairs. Current members at the front of the room." Bella Myer, a red head, pointed to the desks and then to the white board at the front of the room.

Following her instructions, Luke made his way to the back of the room and took a seat by the window. Outside, he could see a few sports teams sharing the field, holding recruitment for their fall teams. Part of him wondered why he hadn't ended up down there, in the gray-green grass, under the grey-blue sky.

But he would always be plagued with the colors. He would be reminded of it wherever he ended up, so he might as well investigate it. He turned back around.

It was only then that he realized that he was surrounded by freshman and sophomores. Ugh. He rolled his eyes and hunched over the desk. He stuck out from this crowd so much that Casper and Bella couldn't possibly miss him if he tried. Why did he decide to do this again?

The current members – there were only 5 of them? – started giving little speeches.

"I'm Bella Myer and I'm the president of the GCA. I'm the one that sent you all the email to be here. I have my colors." There was a sudden rush of murmuring from the freshmen and sophomores. "I've had my colors for 5 years." She made a sweeping motion to her brother.

Casper cleared his throat. "I'm Casper."

A faint inkling of color added to Luke's vision, still not even a wash of color over the usual greyscale. Luke almost growled in frustration.

"I am social secretary; I run the twitter, Facebook, and newsletter, which you will get even when you don't join," he deadpanned.

Luke wasn't sure if he was joking or not, but his sister gave a forced chuckle to fill the pause.

Taking a breath and blinking, Casper finished up, "I do not have my colors but consider myself a strong ally after dealing with my sister and her match for the past 5 years."

Looking to the ground, Luke tried not to feel like he'd been punched in the gut. Why didn't Casper have his colors? Was Luke imagining it? Was he going crazy?

"I'm Billy. I'm just a regular member and I don't have my colors." A hulking guy made a small bow to the room.

A different murmur erupted in the feminine majority of the audience.

"I'm Jesse. I'm the Vice President. I have colors, but not because I found my true mate. I was in an accident when I was younger giving me my colors. I was in the hospital for 3 years afterward, so I don't recommend it." He gave a little smile, an encouraging one.

Part of Luke felt as if Jesse could be a good person to confide in. He had colors but no soulmate, kinda like Luke?

Maybe? Luke had his colors-ish, but he didn't seem to illicit the same thing in his soulmate.

God, this was all kinds of messed up.

Another red head stepped forward from the line-up. She was the last one and seemed to be a ball of energy. "I'm Alex," she gave a little wave, "I'm Bella's true mate, so I've had my colors for 5 years."

More whispering erupted after that. People were hiding their mouths behind their hands and leaning into each other's space. They weren't being sneaky, just secretive.

At the front of the room, Casper's hands balled into fists and his eyebrows furrowed. Honestly, Luke wouldn't have noticed if he hadn't been there specifically to spy on him. Casper's lips twitched twice before he stepped forward, "Now, we're done introducing ourselves. Please," he motioned to the door, "if you were only here for the pizza, leave." He leveled a stare with the now-silent audience.

Even Luke felt guilty under the gaze, even though he hadn't made any comment about Alex and Bella's matching. How could he comment on it? His – albeit unconventional – color match was of the same sex, as well.

19

After a few beats of silence and Bella glaring at Casper from just behind and to the left of him, over half of the audience stood and filed out, silently.

"Now," Casper turned around and picked up a poster tube that had been propped against the wall behind him, "about our club."

Bella heaved a sigh and seemed to resign herself to helping her brother. When he offered her a corner of the poster, she took it and plastered a smile onto her face. "This is the GCA flag."

The poster was flag-shaped. The first half of the flag was divided equally between a white portion and a black portion, while the second half had 6 colored stripes starting with red and ending at violet: a rainbow.

Hopping forward, Alex gestured to the flag. "This side is black and white symbolizing life without colors." She moved to point to the latter side. "Despite that the probably vast majority of you can't see it, this side is multicolored. This stripe is red, then orange, yellow, green, blue, and violet. That side symbolizes life with colors." She gave a broad smile before stepping back in line and tucking her hands behind her back, puffing her chest out with pride.

They must have rehearsed most of the presentation.

Jesse brought his hands together like he was clapping but with no force or sound behind it. "Now, our club isn't a match-making society. Our activities aren't supposed to help you find your match."

It was palpable how much attention from the remaining audience was lost on that sentence. Luke couldn't believe that they were so selfish to think that the club was supposed to help them find their match. But, at the same time, they were freshmen and sophomores.

Come to think of it... It's a good thing Matt hadn't taken a fancy to this society. With his strange obsession with color matches, it was a surprise that he hadn't been interested in the club.

"Mostly what we do is try to organize talks with local university teachers to learn more about color matches and how the color process works and you're more than welcome to attend the lectures without joining the club." He opened his clasped hands to the room. "Any questions?"

Awkward silence filled the room.

Bella took a quick step forward. "So, do any of you have your colors?" She raised her gray-red eyebrows in anticipation.

Suddenly, Luke's elbows felt like lead weight. If he said yes, they'd ask how long and who with or how come and he wasn't ready for that. Instead, he settled for looking around the classroom hoping for other hands.

Unfortunately, every other person was looking around as well.

Huffing in frustration, Luke deposited his chin onto his crossed arms.

"Now that you know how this works, if you want to join, stay and, if you don't want to join, leave." Casper was an absolute ray of sunshine; wasn't he? Wow.

Everyone else collected their things and left.

Billy stepped out of line and took a seat at one of the vacated desks and Alex deflated when the door closed after the last potential member left.

Looking at Luke, Jesse gave a little wave. "Hi! How are you?"

And then all 10 eyes were on him. Actually, that was a lie. 8 eyes were on him. Casper was turned away rolling up the poster and putting it back into the tube.

Clearing his throat, Luke sat straight up. "Uh, good. How are you?"

"Could be better." Jesse offered the same little, encouraging smile as he had before. "What's your name?"

"His name is Luke." Casper said it to the wall but loud enough that it was undeniable. "He lives next door to Bella and me. He's probably here because he thought he had a chance with Bella. Well, you don't." When he turned around, he sent his disdain at Luke through his steely gaze. It took only a few nanoseconds for the look to melt away, though.

Luke was surprised? Embarrassed? Casper was right when he said that Luke was there to see if he had a chance with someone, but it wasn't Bella. Luke settled on hurt; what had he done to Casper that made him think so low of him?

Taking a sudden step forward, Casper reached a hand in Luke's direction, simply a gesture since they were on opposite sides of the room. "I'm sorry. I'm just-" He brought a hand up to scrub down his face. "People don't usually join, and, when they do, they've always had... ulterior motives."

"Nah, man, it's, uh... it's cool." Luke tried to look anywhere but Casper, but the hints of color all over the room only replaced the thought of Casper to the forefront of his brain. He remedied the situation by closing his eyes. "I just wanted to join to, uh, to learn more about it. My parents had an unconventional color match and that sort of thing can be genetic so... yeah." Some of it was absolute bullshit. His mother never talked about her and Jack's color match; but the genetic thing was straight from the Staged Color Progression Wikipedia page.

Billy swiveled in his seat. "I say if Mr. Grumps hasn't scared you away that you're perfect GCA member material." He reached his hand out across the desk that separated the front and back rows. "Welcome to the club."

Rocking up out of the chair, Luke grabbed his hand and gave a quick shake. "Nice to meet you."

"How about we pull the desks together a bit and discuss some of the upcoming events?" Bella started nudging a desk and chair at the front row.

Jesse swung a gangly leg over a chair and jerked it and the accompanying desk around. "Sounds good to me." While the others took seats and moved the tables into an impromptu, organic shape, Jesse turned to Luke. "Are you planning on joining any other clubs? We're not a really strict club, but some of the others are."

Nodding along, Luke trained his eyes on Jesse, ignoring the clattering from the rest of the members. "I was thinking of joining the Engineering and Robotics Team." He shrugged.

"Oh, I'm on that," Alex exclaimed. "As long as you have a good record with math and physics, you're a sure thing. It's a good club, but it only really has meetings in March and April just before the Robotics Tournament." Alex sent Luke a thumbs up where she'd draped herself backwards over a chair near Billy.

Casper took a seat next to Luke, though, he didn't look at Luke or pay him any mind at all.

Swallowing the awkward bubbling in his throat, Luke looked to the other members of the club and nodded to them. They seemed like nice people and he didn't have any friends. What did he have to lose? "Cool." He nodded and turned toward Casper whose head was bent over a printed agenda for the meeting. Luke repeated, "Cool."

Chapter 3:

Giving Thanks

School had gotten out early since it was the day before Thanksgiving Break. Casper had argued that they should still meet this week and Alex had offered her house after school. Luke had never been there before, so Casper pointed the way from his passenger seat.

"Take a left up here and it's the third house on the right."

Luckily for Luke, Casper had warmed up to him a bit. Somewhere between Luke not trying to date his sister and taking Casper's side in arguments, they'd become friends. And Luke could be happy with that. The colors had stopped progressing as quickly. Instead of getting more colors every time he saw Casper, he might get some each week, more likely every two weeks or so.

The color was now strong enough that Luke could see the blue of Casper's eyes across the room, but at the same time he couldn't see the different yellows and oranges of the falling leaves. They either looked yellow or red, with nothing in between. It made some activities extremely annoying, like watching low-budget sitcoms.

He was pretty sure it wouldn't be that annoying if he had all of his colors and he wouldn't even bat an eye if he was watching in greyscale. It was just this awkward in between that made it so frustrating. And worse than that, he had no one to complain too. He was still just a Grey Ally in the club and he wasn't sure how to go about telling his mom or anyone about it.

It just wasn't normal. It meant he was broken. They may even tell him to go to a doctor or something and Luke really didn't like doctors so... he'd decided to take his chances with frustration management.

Casper made a beeline to Alex's door and rang the bell. Luke chuckled, opening the back door of the ambassador to get the two casserole dishes and a bowl. It was Thanksgiving, so they had brought food.

When Luke had told his mother, she had given him the whole kitchen the night before and ordered pizza for their

27

dinner. Luke liked to cook. Part of him couldn't wait to have a family of his own that he could cook for, but that thought came with a one-way ticket to the section of his brain that had become dedicated to Casper, where he catalogued his favorite foods and animals and fonts. By the way, they were honey buns and burgers, bees and cats, and Helvetica.

Anyway, Luke brought a bread pudding sort of thing that tasted like honey buns, some homemade mac and cheese, and a 7-layer bean dip. Jesse had said he'd get chips and Luke had made sure to tell him to bring some of the tortilla variety. Jesse had pointed finger-guns at Luke with a quick 'You got it!'

Luke lit at Casper's side at the door. "So, Alex and Bella are already here?"

"Yeah. Alex wanted to get everything cleaned up, so they left right at the bell." He glanced at Luke holding all of the dishes and quickly grabbed one. "Sorry, forgot you brought so much food." He tried to peek into the casserole carrier he'd taken.

Nudging him with his elbow, Luke tutted at him. "No peeking. It's a Thanksgiving surprise." He flashed a grin.

Casper lowered his hands and the casserole carrier to his knees. "I don't like surprises."

"I know, but you'll like at least one of these dishes. I can guarantee it." He winked. Was he flirting? If he was, he needed to stop.

Luckily the door opened before Luke could say anything more. Bella pushed the screen door out and waved them in. "Come on in. Alex's setting up the basement. You can put the food on the ping pong table for now." She pointed to a door leading to a set of stairs going down.

"Aren't you coming?"

"No, you and Luke go down. I just got a text from Jesse saying that he's turning onto Sycamore Drive, so I'm going to wait to let him in."

"Okay."

Luke waited until Casper had caught up to him at the door to the basement before making his way down.

The basement was set up almost like an arcade and Luke thought he might swoon. There were two arcade game kiosks – Pac-Man and Galaga, a ping pong table, an air hockey table, and a huge television complete with a Blu-ray player and an Xbox.

Leaving the dishes on the ping pong table as instructed, Luke moved to look around the room. There was a big comfy sectional sofa centered in front of the television and at least 5 full shelves of DVDs, Blu-rays, and Xbox Games. "This is like heaven."

"It's a bit dark to be heaven." Casper's quip was almost immediate.

Luke had learned that this was Casper's sense of humor, and, honestly, it was pretty funny in the right environment. He shot a 'I get it' grin in Casper's direction.

"It gets pretty bright once we get this baby turned on." Alex popped her head up from the other side of the sofa. She was sitting on the floor with batteries and Xbox controllers. "It's kinda like a movie theatre."

"Well, I like it." Luke circled around to the other side of the couch and took a seat next to Alex on the floor. "So, what are our game options?" He reached toward the stack of Xbox games. "Oh cool, you have Supernatural? That only came out last month!" He flipped over the case and read the inscription.

Alex popped out old batteries from a clear Xbox controlled and grabbed new ones from the pack to her left. "It's good, but you can tell that the developers didn't have their colors yet; well, you can't but I can. The color balance is off. You can have it if you want." She smiled at him. "I just can't play it, you know?"

Grip loosening on the game, Luke suddenly had a picture of the game with opposing solid colors and could feel himself grow nauseous. If someone with all of their colors couldn't handle it, he couldn't stand a chance. "Thanks, Alex, but I couldn't." He put it back on the pile. "If you can't play it, why is it in the pile?"

She shrugged collecting the remaining batteries and standing up. "I'm not the only person playing. I thought maybe you or Casper or Billy might enjoy it." She left, presumably, to put the batteries away, maybe to check on Bella too.

It was times like this that Luke really wished that his colors had come all the way in. He'd been looking forward to the game for almost a year, but now he wouldn't be able to enjoy it. It fucking sucked.

"It's not very good. You can only play as a supernatural hunter. The characters have limited storyline and the graphics for the female characters are much worse than for the male characters." Casper took a seat behind Luke on the sectional. He leaned back into the overstuffed cushions. "The company has been advertising a sequel game where you can play as hunters, angels, or demons. Personally, I'm waiting for that one. Although, I'm not entirely sure if they'll fix the female graphics or color balance."

Luke nodded. "So, you like video games?" Luke turned sideways to better look at Casper while he talked.

Shrugging, Casper seemed to sink further into the couch. "I play them for a while then I forget about them for a while."

That made sense with everything else Luke knew about Casper. And, just like everything else about him, the new information was filed away in that Casper-only section of Luke's thoughts.

"And the party has started!" Jesse jumped down the last two steps of the basement stairs and held up 6 different bags of chips. "And, yes, I remembered the tortilla chips."

Billy snorted. "Yeah, he remembered them when I was driving past the grocery store, so we had to stop and get some." He threw his coat over the back of the sofa and poked at one of the casserole dish carriers. "What other food do we have?"

Waving her hands in the air, Bella entered the room with Alex close behind her. "All will be revealed soon enough, so everyone gather around." She took Jesse's hand in one of hers and Alex's in the other.

Casper stood and offered a hand to Luke to help him up, which Luke took. And, much to Luke's emotional distress, he didn't let go of his hand as he led him the short distance to the amoebic circle. Luke's other hand was shaking a little when he took hold of Alex's free hand.

"I want each of us to say one thing that we're thankful for," Bella said, "I'll go first." She took a breath and closed her eyes. Alex took the hint and closed her eyes too, so did Casper, Billy, and Jesse. That just left Luke, looking at Casper with no one able to catch him doing it.

Since they were holding hands, Luke was close enough to see Casper's lashes, individually hitting his high cheekbones. Luke really hoped that Casper would turn out to be his color match, even if it took a while; he just wanted to be able to look at him like this more often.

Another inkling of color tinged into Luke's vision.

With that, Luke gave a silent huff and closed his eyes.

"I am thankful for 5 years of colors and for my wonderful match. I'm thankful that it worked out this well and that we can all be friends and part of this club."

Alex came next. "I am thankful for... ditto, just ditto." She squeezed Luke's hand.

He panicked and just squeezed Casper's hand immediately. He didn't know what to say; what was he supposed to say? Casper squeezed back like he was telling him that he forgot to say something, but Luke just squeezed harder; he wasn't ready yet.

Sighing, Casper finally took the cue. "I am thankful for my sister, my family, my friends. I'm thankful that our school is so open and inviting."

Then Jesse's, "I'm thankful that Luke and Billy brought food. I'm looking forward to eating it." There was a mixture of light groans and hushed laughing.

"I'm thankful for good friends, good food, and good times." Billy ended.

At that point, both Alex and Casper squeezed Luke's hands. Luke cleared his throat. "Uh, I'm thankful for my family? I'm thankful for meeting all of you?" He though quickly. "I, uh, I'm thankful not to be alone for my senior year."

Everything was quiet for a moment. Luke was expecting something, either an 'amen' or a really loud sneeze; nothing came though. Everyone just let go of hands and Luke was forced to open his eyes. Everyone was wearing little smiles at each other and there was a permeating warm feeling pooling in the center of their group.

Jesse was the first to turn out of the circle. "Well, I'm starving." He grabbed a grey-orange paper plate and pulled open one of the chip bags. He loaded two handfuls onto his plate and popped one into his mouth. "Okay, unveil the food!"

Unzipping the first casserole dish, Luke revealed his mac and cheese. Billy peeled back some aluminum foil from another dish to show off his baked ziti. Bella opened a store-bought veggie tray followed closely by fruit tray.

"Did you make it from scratch?" Alex's pupils might as well have been hearts. Her fork was already in the mac and cheese. She took the forkful to her mouth instead of her plate and moaned, loudly. Bella swept in after her, putting a serving spoon into the mac and cheese.

Luke nodded. "Yeah. My mom gave me the whole kitchen yesterday. I also made 7-layer dip." He plucked at the saran wrap on the bowl.

"Is this honey-bun casserole?" Casper's voice filtered through the sounds of food and cheeriness. He was looking at Luke with anticipation with only half of the zipper undone on the casserole caddy.

Trying not to blush, Luke tried not to swallow his tongue. "Uh-huh. I thought you'd enjoy it."

A full-blown grin stretched across Casper's face. "Thank you, Luke." He dug into the casserole loading his plate with it. He didn't even get anything else before he went to take his seat on the couch.

Chapter 4:

When We Grow Up

"Can we skip next week's meeting?" Alex groaned into the table where she'd practically melted. "I think I'll need the time to study for my English exam. Who wants to help me read three of Shakespeare's plays by next Thursday?" She turned a pleading look at Bella.

Bella simply shook her head. "I'm already helping you study for History and I have my own classes, too. I can't help you catch up on an entire semester of poor time-management."

"It wasn't poor time-management. I managed to complete a video game or a multi-faceted, World of Warcraft quest every week. I'd say my time-management skills are top-notch."

Casper shuffled his papers. "Yeah, it's your prioritizing that needs improvement."

Honestly, Luke couldn't be blamed for how loud he laughed at that. It was perfect timing and it was absolutely hilarious. Everyone else, those who weren't laughing, just didn't have the right kind of humor, okay?

Glaring at him, Alex stuck out her bottom lip like she was truly upset by Luke's laugh.

"What?" Luke shrugged. "He totally compared you to Hermione." He peeked at her from the corner of his eye. "She needs to sort out her priorities," he quoted in a very fake British accent.

Just as he'd hoped, her pout slid away and a little shimmer of awe replaced it. She grinned a little and returned to her normally happy self. She reached to the edge of her desk, wrapped her hands around the far side, shrugged, and settled into a contented posture.

"I have my English exam on Thursday, too. I'd much prefer to have the extra time to study." Jesse added. His head was bent over his lap, but he darted his eyes around as if he expected people to be mad at him.

Bella nodded slowly and turned to Casper. Casper just stared back.

Making an over dramatic eyeroll, Bella huffed out an exasperated breath of air. "Look, Casper, if you want to meet by yourself in this room, be my guest, but I think we're gonna give some leeway next week." She turned squinted eyes toward Alex. "Some leeway," she repeated at the younger red-head.

Alex seemed happy enough with that though; her face broke into a grin. "Thank you," it was almost a sing-song. "I don't even understand why I have to take English tests if I'm going to be a computer programmer or game designer. I mean, I know how to read and write; at this point, they're just making me read old books and talk about my feelings with a bunch of strangers."

"You've had classes with these people all year, and probably last year and the year before that and before that..." As Billy trailed off, he leaned back in his chair and slid his butt forward on the seat. For a moment, Luke wondered if he was doing to slide straight to the floor, but he didn't.

Reshuffling his papers and drawing the attention of the room back to him, Casper leveled a look with Alex. "Not exactly the case for Alex. How many years have you skipped again?"

Silence fell. Luke looked between the two. Casper was calm and collected but Alex's cheeks were approaching a red that would match her hair color.

Tired of waiting, Casper continued, "4 years, right?"

Alex's face got even redder, but she managed to nod.

"Stop embarrassing her." Bella threw a pink eraser at her brother. "How would you like if I advertised what year of school you're supposed to be in?"

Nothing against Alex's accomplishment – actually it was super impressive and Luke felt a little pang of pity? Guilt? Matt would probably have skipped some grades if they hadn't been moving around so much – but Luke was a lot more interested in the information about Casper. He tried to nonchalantly direct all of his attention at Casper.

While Casper hadn't gotten red like Alex, he had gotten a lot stiller. Luke had learned to tell when Casper was embarrassed. He froze up, he stopped what he's doing, or he stared into the distance. The Casper-section of his brain was pinging in the background of his thoughts.

Wait, was Casper younger than him?

"Bella-"

"Don't 'Bella' me." She crossed her arms over her chest and kicked one leg up to cross it over the other. "Go ahead and share with the class."

Casper's papers were jittering in his hands. He really didn't seem to want to talk about it.

Clearing his throat, Luke leaned forward. "So, Alex, you want to be a computer scientist? Where did you apply for college? Anywhere local?"

The tension in the air didn't immediately dissipate, but it was thinning, slowly.

"I applied everywhere, but I worked especially hard on the applications for the local colleges and whatever ones that Bella applied to." She sent a smile toward her color match.

With that gesture, Bella's stand-off with her brother eased and she uncrossed her legs; her arms sagged into her lap. "Yeah, I'm really hoping for this one med school in California. They have a brand-new lab-only building that looks like something out of... Which one was it?"

"Star Trek," Alex supplied.

"Yeah that." Bella's eyes glazed over a little while she talked about her top choice for school.

Luke's attention shifted though; it fell back onto Casper. Since Luke had changed the topic, Casper's shoulders had sagged back down to their normal level and he had carefully trained his gaze to the desk in front of him. Not sure what to do, Luke reached over and put his hand on Casper's thigh, giving a light squeeze.

Jerking a little, Casper's eyes flashed to the hand on his thigh before relaxing even further than before. He turned a grateful smile in Luke's direction.

Another smudge of color tinged Luke's vision, but he couldn't be frustrated in that moment. He was just happy that he could help Casper.

Retracting his hand, Luke didn't know where to put it. It was warm from Casper's thigh and he kind of wanted to cherish the feeling. He ended up awkwardly resting his forearm to his own thigh, letting his warmed and tingling hand hang limp between his knees.

By the time Luke tuned back into the conversation, Billy was talking.

"Speak for yourself," he waved a hand at Jesse, "I want to be a cook, a chef; I don't need any of this." He gestured around in a vague move meant to signify the classroom or the school or something. "My food may look horrible for a while, but it will taste divine."

Jesse crossed his arms over his chest. "Don't worry, a lot of food looks ugly."

It was true. And worst part for Luke was that he couldn't complain about it. But, some food looked absolutely nasty in color; his mom's split pea soup looked like some sort of green-grey-brown slop. He'd always thought it was bright green, but no. At least burgers still looked good. And pie.

Elbowing Casper in the side, Jesse waggled an eyebrow. "So, what do you want to be?"

"He's gonna be a doctor like Bella." Alex provided with pride. "My family is brilliant!" She sent warm smiles to Bella and Casper.

A pang rang through Luke. Her family? Well, in a way, they were, and, in a significant way, they still weren't. Alex was basically a part of the Myer family. She and Bella would get married one day and make it official, but it was basically a done deal. She was Casper's sister-in-law already.

43

Did that mean she was Luke's sister-in-law? He was Casper's color match, right? Maybe?

Luke realized that he really wouldn't mind being family with Alex or Bella. And, truth be told, he already considered himself Casper's family, whether the feeling was mutual or not remained to be seen.

It probably wasn't.

Sighing, Luke picked at a scratch on the edge of the wooden desk top. He'd thought himself into a bad mood. He hated when he did that.

"Don't you need colors to do anything in the Sciences? You have to take Chemistry and Biology and stuff and that requires colors." Billy sounded like he regretted saying it while he was saying it.

Casper took a big, steadying breath and picked at his pants leg. "I'm hoping that my grades and academic standing will make me eligible for the Grey Scholarship Foundation for the Medical Sciences."

"What's that?" Luke asked automatically; his brain was soaking in the information and cataloging it accordingly.

"In short, it's a huge scholarship. It's for students who show a high aptitude for the sciences that don't yet have their colors. Statistics show that most people find their color match by the time they're 23 and only begin their collegiate education after that. The Sciences are hard subjects to take long breaks from. The scholarship covers the special materials, books, and ClearColor glasses for its recipients."

Everyone sat in silence for a long moment.

"ClearColor glasses are really expensive." Luke said. "I..." Luke couldn't say it out loud. He wished he could fix them, him and Casper. He wished he could give his colors to Casper. He wished that they had met and they'd both gotten colors at the same time. He wished that everything had gone to plan like in the romance novels that he swears he doesn't take from his mother's bookcase. "I hope you get it." In that moment, Luke felt tired, absolutely exhausted.

The club bell rang letting all of the meeting clubs know that the late buses would be leaving in 15 minutes. Everyone stood from their seats.

Jesse and Billy waved their goodbyes and made their way to the door. They took the buses most days. Jesse's family had a car that he could use, but only with good reason. Billy usually just walked to his job when he needed to and didn't want the hassle of a car.

Alex saluted at Luke, winking too. "See you later." She grabbed Bella's wrist and tugged her toward the door too.

"Aren't you going to help put the tables back?" Casper called after them.

Bella called back, somewhat apologetically. "Not today, sorry. I owe you one." They were out the door already.

"Must be having a date or something." Luke shifted the desk he had occupied before moving on to the others in the circle. "They don't usually skip out on the clean-up." He offered Casper a smile, trying to apologize for Alex's behavior. They were family-ish after all.

Staring after them, Casper stood still. "I wish I understood what it was like."

"Hm?"

"What it was like to have a color match? Does it feel different than just having friends or liking people?"

Luke gave a vague shoulder shrug. In his experience, it felt like something special. It felt like he was Casper's best friend and brother and confidant and side-kick. It felt like he was supposed to keep Casper safe but also that Casper was supposed to keep him safe in return. Did it feel like that for everyone?

Head aching a little, Luke shifted Casper's desk back into the usual formation. He stood next to Casper for a moment. Casper was still looking where his sister and her color match had left them. Luke wanted to know what else was going through his head, but that was unlikely to happen.

"Uh, Casper, can I ask you something?"

Casper turned his eyes from the door. This close, Luke could see the blue in his eyes. It was grey-blue, but Luke wasn't sure if that was because he couldn't see just color or if that steely blue was the final color. Either way, Luke's throat became dry and he couldn't look away.

His grey-pink lips moved. "I think you just did. But, you can ask me another."

Nodding a little, Luke tried to find his thoughts again. "What grade are you supposed to be in?"

Casper tilted his head to the side and his features softened. "I thought you were going to ask me something worse." He shook his head a little, like he was relieved, maybe? "I was held back a year. I had a tough time when my father left. Bella had Alex to keep her stable; I..." he sighed.

The room felt much smaller than a minute earlier; the space had previously been empty with six people, yet, at that moment, it felt too small for two.

"You didn't," Luke supplied softly. He wasn't sure where it came from, but he offered Casper an encouraging grin. "Color matches aren't the only people you can share with. Your friends will support you too; I'll support you."

"Thank you, Luke."

Chapter 5:

Feeling Blue

Luke was almost asleep, that was how exhausted he was. He was already done with his college applications and all of that work, and truth, he was very happy with that fact. But since the high school faculty also knew that the college application process was over, they were laying on the work. He had three essays, two research papers, a group project and presentation, and an experiment report due in the next week and a half. On top of all that, it was high time for the Engineering and Robotics Team, which he had joined earlier in the year, and both clubs were getting ready for the Spring Fling.

But then it would be the sweet bliss of Spring Break.

He was counting the days, possibly the hours, until then.

Correction, he was counting when he wasn't half-asleep, like the way he was at that moment, slumped over a desk in the GCA's club meeting room.

He wasn't entirely sure why they even had to participate in the Spring Fling. It seemed like a lost cause. The club would be disbanded if they didn't win over at least 5 students to carry it forward. All of the current members were seniors and moving on to bigger and better things. Although, Matt already said that he'd like to join if they could keep it going.

Luke hadn't been very enthused at the news, but Casper had politely thanked him for his willingness.

The desperate state of the club, however, had kick-started their participation in the Spring Fling, a Friday event just before the start of Spring Break. Luke didn't remember it at any other school he'd been to, and he'd been to quite a few. It was a day that the clubs could advertise to students from the middle schools. Buses would bring middle schoolers over to participate in games, demonstrations, and meetings.

Having no idea of what to expect, Luke hadn't been able to offer any helpful ideas or suggestions.

In the end, they decided to make a tri-fold information board, give out bags of skittles at their table, and sign up for a slot in each of the two formal presentations for the day.

Alex and Jesse had come up with the worst and only idea for what they should do for the formal presentations: skits.

So, in the end, Luke, Billy, and Alex were trying to pick costumes for the club members' characters from outfits each of them brought in while everyone else sought out study help because of all of the pre-Spring-Break assignments.

Part of Luke wondered if he could have gone to the library and taken a nap in one of the comfy chairs while he waited for Casper to be ready to head home, but Casper would ask him about the club meeting and Luke wouldn't be able to lie to Casper, so it would go downhill very quickly and he wasn't prepared to deal with that... So, he was nodding off in the club room instead.

"Luke!" Alex must've been trying to get his attention for a while. "Which one for Bella?"

He lolled his head in her direction to look at her and the options. She was frazzled; her red-gray hair was mostly fly-aways. He lolled back to his half-asleep position. "The yellow one."

The tapping of Billy's heel stopped and the room became deathly still.

It took Luke a long moment with his absolute exhaustion to realize his mistake. His eyes flew open and he pushed up into a fully sitting position. Slowly, he turned around to see his friends, hopefully confidants?

"You can see colors?" Alex's face was devoid of emotion.

Billy's was screwed up with confusion before it morphed into a grimace. "You can see colors?"

"No?" It was worth the shot. Was it worth the shot?

Alex looked upset, like Luke had wounded her. Billy's eyebrows twitched further together at the top of his nose.

"Yes?" Luke tried again.

No one did anything for a long moment. The only sound in the room was the clock ticking; Luke wasn't even sure if anyone was breathing. The longer the silence went, the louder his heart seemed to pound. Could they hear it?

Alex fell back into the chair beneath her. Her hands dropped to the desk, the options she'd been holding up seemingly forgotten. "You can see colors. Have you been able to see colors the whole school year?" She was staring at the wood-grain top of the desk.

Unsure of whether Alex was speaking to herself or to him, Luke flicked his eyes to Billy only to be met with a stern look. "Fuck you, this is a safe space. That's literally what the GCA is for. Why the- why the fuck did you keep that a secret?"

Heart sinking, Luke knew this was it; he couldn't go back from this. That comfy chair in the library seemed a lot more tempting now. "I, I uh..."

"Do you not trust us?"

"We are the people you would tell that to."

"I mean, I know you're new, but I think we've been welcoming."

"We have been welcoming, Alex. Don't be hard on yourself."

"Yeah, well, don't be hard on him!"

"Guys!" Luke found his voice again. He really didn't want to see these people arguing, especially over something as dumb as Luke being an idiot. "I have colors, but I also don't have colors...?" He looked between the two of them.

Alex watched with wide eyes, completely open and sympathetic. Billy made up for it, though, he was snarling, like if Luke got too close, he'd bite.

They were waiting for him to explain and, honestly, Luke didn't know how to do that. He wasn't sure where to start. He wasn't an expert on these things like Dr. Arlow was. Oh, okay, he could start there.

"So, uh, you remember the talk we went to last month at the University of Missouri? With Dr. Arlow?" Luke curled his hands into fists on the desktop.

They nodded, Billy's harsher than Alex's.

"Okay, remember when he went into the stuff on abnormal psycolorgy? How some color matches don't have it very lucky, that they may meet too early or too late, that it takes a long time for one's colors to come in. All that? So, I have – or I think I have – Staged Color Progression. Dr. Arlow went over it briefly. It's when someone starts getting their colors but it takes forever to have them come all the way in. So, I can see color, but I can still see grayscale." He brought the heels of his hands to his eyes. He was so exhausted, he couldn't tell if any of this made sense or not. "Ugh, I'm explaining this wrong." Luke slumped over so his elbows were propped on the desk.

Slowly, Billy's foot began to tap again in the background. "So, you can see some colors, like blue but not red?"

Luke didn't look up when he responded, he still felt agonizingly guilty over all of this. "Not really? It's like I can see grayscale with color at a really low opacity over it." He debated briefly with himself before adding, "Every once in a while, the opacity gets darker, like I can see more of the color and less of the grayscale."

"So, you get a little more every time you see your soulmate? So, they have all their colors?" Alex said it lightly, like if she spoke too strong or too seriously, she would break reality. Luke wasn't sure if that was possible, but, at that moment, it felt as if it was.

Peeking up, Luke was surprised to find Alex was a little flushed. He realized in that moment just how much more color he had than the last time he'd been around blushing people. Wow.

Also, he totally picked up on Alex using 'they'. Part of him was relieved, but another part of him was preoccupied on being worried about how much she knew, about how obvious he'd been.

Billy had calmed down, too. He seemed like he was still processing, but he wasn't fuming anymore and that was a step in the right direction. "She must be pretty, right?"

Letting out a long exhale, Luke tried to figure out how to word the next part. He wasn't really sure what their views on same-sex color matches were. Like, Alex was probably pretty cool with it, since she was one half of a same-sex match, but Billy...? Well, Billy was cool with Alex and Bella, obviously... but, also there were guys that were cool with girl-girl matches but squeamish about boy-boy because they're male and that's dumb but-

"Oof," Billy grunted and rubbed his side where Alex had elbowed him.

She pointed a glare in his direction and a little light seemed to flicker on behind his eyes. "Or, uh, he. I mean, he must be pretty, er... handsome? I just mean, whoever it is must look good. You know what I mean, right?"

Luke could have kissed Alex or, at least, her gaydar? "Well, uh, he, uh..." This was awkward even with their extra support. "His colors didn't come in at all." Luke's eyes flicked around looking for something to focus on; he ended up staring at the discarded clothes on Alex's desk.

A short silence fell again.

56

"That's sad." Alex's voice had taken on an empathetic ring. "I wish there was something I could do. I couldn't imagine if…" She trailed off, but Luke knew what she had been saying. She couldn't imagine if it were her in his position, if Bella hadn't gotten her colors when Alex had.

"So, you're gay?" Billy's voice was basically normal again.

Luke huffed and turned playfully annoyed eyes on his friend. "I never really thought of it like that. I mean, most people are just looking for their soulmate, right? They're soulmate-sexual?"

"But, I mean, how long have you figured that it might be a guy?" Billy leaned forward on the desk, getting closer to Luke as if he was waiting to be told a secret.

Thinking back, Luke couldn't really come up with an exact moment. He shrugged, "My mother always jokes that when I comforted her after my dad died I promised her not to marry a man like him." Belatedly, Luke realized that he hadn't exactly explained that his father hadn't just died but had died in a drunk-driving accident. Hopefully, they'd take the statement for what it was and let that other discussion alone for another time. He wasn't sure how much more of these serious conversations he could take.

Alex snickered. "That's adorable. I'm sorry. I shouldn't laugh. It's just... so fucking adorable."

In retaliation, Luke threw her the stink-eye, and, when he heard Billy's snickers, he threw him the finger. And after a moment of choked off chuckles, they all burst out laughing.

The pressure in the room evaporated and Luke felt like a weight had been lifted off his chest.

"So, are you going to tell us who he is?" Alex waggled her eyebrow. And just like that, the weight landed right back in Luke's ribcage. His horror must have shown on his face because Alex hands flew up and started waving back and forth. "Nevermind, nevermind. Another day, maybe?"

"Maybe," Luke agreed.

"So," Billy poked at the clothes on Alex's desk, "do you think we can decide the rest of the outfits before the late bus bell?" He looked over at the clock. "We have fifteen minutes."

Alex shot up and gathered the clothes. "Bella will have my head if I don't at least have this done. So, what? We decided on the yellow one for her. Now, which of these for Casper?" She threw the approved outfit in the approved pile and slid the other one back into the grocery bag it had originally come out of. She pulled out two other grocery bags showing off the clothes that Casper had brought in as possible outfits for his character.

Without hesitation, Luke immediately said, "The blue one."

Chapter 6:

Bella's Birthday

"I have to thank your mother."

"Why?" Luke led the way up to his room. "You've already thanked her twice and Bella brought over 'Thank You' cookies yesterday." He pivoted on the stair for a moment and pointed finger-guns at her. "Which are awesome, by the way."

Alex beamed. "She's a great baker." She leaned forward and cupped a hand around a side of her mouth and whispered, "Just don't ask her to cook."

Laughing, Luke hopped up the last few stairs and pushed open the door to his room. At this point, Alex was like family. It was strange how easily she fit into his life. Of course, part of Luke wondered if that was due to the fact that they were sort-of destined kind-of to be in-laws, maybe?

But that was something that Luke didn't want to think about at the moment.

Bella's birthday was Sunday and her party was tomorrow, Saturday. Casper and Bella's mother, Sharon, was very strict about Alex coming over. It was one of the reasons they usually hung out elsewhere. Luke had only been to Casper's house twice in the entire year.

At first, he'd seen it as a bit of an insult; hell, he was Casper's best friend. But, when he found out that Alex was invited over about as often (and, at this point, rarely took up the offer), he felt a bit better.

"So, you can either sleep on the trundle bed that we'd have to pull out of Matt's room or you can take my bed and I'll sleep in my brother's room." Luke pointed to the door across from his.

Alex dumped her stuff on Luke's bed. "Whatever you want. It's your house, not mine." She looked around his room. "Well, maybe it's your house. Why don't you have more stuff in your room?"

Shrugging, Luke sat on the edge of his bed. "We've never stayed anywhere long enough for me to accumulate anything." He looked around; it felt cold and impersonal, but he kind of liked it that way. It was almost clinical. And, in a weird way, it reminded him of Casper and Casper's room. One of the times he'd been at the Myer house, he'd been given the grand tour, and, while the laundry room and the pantry were interesting in their own right, the highlights for Luke had been Casper's room and the kitchen.

When Luke's eyes landed back on Alex, she was wearing a smirk and had her fists pressed into her hips. "So," she raised an eyebrow, "if I were to, oh I don't know, go look in Matt's room, it would be just as bare as this?"

Luke rolled his eyes and flopped back onto the bed, defeated. "What do you want me to say? That I like it like this?" He threw his arms out, gesturing to his room in general.

The bed dipped and Luke knew that Alex had sat, too. "I mean, if that's the truth, then yeah." Her voice was serious again. "I like the idea of you being truthful with me?"

"Is that a question?"

"No?"

"Is that?"

"Luke." Alex flopped back next to him, narrowly missing her bags on the way down. "I don't know much about you. I mean, I met you less than a year ago, but it's weird. It's like, ugh, this is going to sound dumb, but, my colors have seemed more vibrant since you got here."

Luke's brain blanked as he stared at the ceiling. He thought this would be more awkward. A girl, admittedly a very gay girl, who was Matt's age, was laying on his bed with him, saying that he made her colors more vibrant. But, it was the most normal thing in the world. It was nice having someone to talk to about colors and color matches and same-sex color matches.

"God. I sound crazy, don't I?" She pressed a hand to her face.

"Not really," Luke shrugged into his comforter, "I mean, you know that my colors are coming in slowly and that every time I see someone they get brighter. Maybe that can happen after you find your match, too?"

She flipped over onto her stomach and tucked her elbows under her head. "I didn't really think of it like that." She sighed. "I didn't think there was any more color to get after I met Bella."

63

"Did you tell her?"

Alex's eyes snapped wide open. "Of course, I did! I tell Bella everything."

Luke tensed. "Everything?"

Sagging, Alex's eyes turned down to the comforter. She used a finger to trace one of the lines of stitches. "I didn't tell her about your colors. That seemed too personal." She flopped to her side. "Gosh, and it's killing me. I haven't kept a secret from Bella EVER! I feel so guilty."

And that made Luke feel guilty. It was bad enough that he was keeping a secret, but the fact that he was making other people keep his secret was taxing. "I'm sorry." It was barely a whisper.

"No, no. It's okay, Luke. I mean, I'm your friend and I want to be there for you. When you decide to tell them, I'll be there with you." She patted his shoulder twice.

He was never going to tell them, Bella or Casper or any of the Miltons. He'd decided that months ago, but now he had the growing guilt of Alex's confidence to contend with.

Wait, was Alex a Myer? Had he already broken his own resolve?

At one of the talks the GCA went to, a lecturer, Dr. Talley, had explained how some people can know each other as children and have no chemical attraction or color match, but, when they meet again later in life, sparks fly and their colors come in.

Maybe that would happen to Casper. Maybe Luke just had to be patient.

At the end of the lecture, Luke had asked the professor about Staged Color Progression, but Dr. Talley hadn't been very useful. He'd simply pointed him to the next lecturer in the series, Dr. Arlow. But whatever. Luke had a working theory and he was going with it, whether it was scientifically plausible or not.

He just really hoped it was.

"So," Alex said awkwardly, "I brought a color game. Do you want to try playing?"

Luke's eyes darted to his door. "Yeah, definitely, just let me close the door."

They ended up sitting cross-legged across from each other on the bed, each with a fan of cards. Since Luke could see the grayscale and the colors, he could tell why people without their colors couldn't play. All of the cards were the exact same gray; the hues were different colors, but the gray was the same.

These were games that people would play with other married, color-match couples or as children, after or before they saw in grayscale. Luke remembered, vaguely, that he had played these games with his mother when he was little. He hadn't had a chance to play them with Matt since he'd lost his colors before Matt had been old enough to play.

Come to think of it, his mom and Matt hadn't played the games when Matt had been old enough to play them. At least, Luke couldn't think of any time they'd played. Maybe it reminded his mom of when his father was alive.

"Your turn." Alex sing-songed through Luke's thoughts. She was winning, so she was in a fantastic mood.

Laughing, Luke shook his head and stared at the last discard. He sighed a little. "Is that green closer to blue or yellow?" He tried to really concentrate on the card. If he'd been paying attention, he'd know whether blue or yellow was more recently played and then obviously know which end of the green-spectrum it was on. There was a logic to it, blue, blue-green, yellow-green, then yellow and so on.

No wonder Alex was winning.

"It's blue-green." Her happy expression didn't change, but the chime in her voice did. She sounded like she was pitying him, just a little. "So, you still can't see that much color, huh?"

He shrugged. "I can see enough. I can tell that it's green, but the gray behind it makes it hard to tell if it leans toward blue or yellow. I have the same problem with purple and orange."

"So, you can see primary and secondary colors but not tertiary or anything else."

Luke placed a blue card down on the pile. "Yeah, basically."

She quickly placed a purple card, logically a blue-purple, and then waited for Luke again. Luke stared into his hand. He had three purple cards, but he didn't know if they were blue-purple or red-purple. He pulled one out and showed it to Alex with a raised eyebrow. She shook her head. So, that one must have been blue-purple since he couldn't play it. He put it close to his green cards in his hand to remind himself.

For Luke, it was turning into a memory game.

He tried comparing that card with the other two purple cards, but he couldn't see enough of a difference to make a guess. Sighing, he picked up the next one. When Alex nodded at him, he grinned and put it down. That card must have been red-purple.

Alex quickly laid another purple card, logically blue-purple.

Busy glaring at the last unclassified purple card in his hand, Luke jumped when his door burst open.

"Alex! There you are! Can I ask you a question about color matches?" Matt stood in the doorway, holding a book to his chest; a finger was tucked between two of its pages, probably marking where his question came from.

Luke growled, "Knock, bitch," but his brain jump-started into trying to hide the cards. Since Matt had startled them both, the discard and draw piles were a mess on the bed and Alex had dropped her cards in surprise. Luke tried to gather up the cards.

Jumping up from the bed and walking toward Matt, Alex grinned. "Of course, Matt." She tried to sequester him to the door. "What's your question?"

The two of them got along really well, too, and, for that, Luke was very grateful. In previous places, Luke had made friends that Matt had hated and Matt had made friends that Luke had hated. Nina. God, Luke had hated Nina.

It seemed to help that Matt and Alex were the same age and both too smart for their own good.

Matt's squinted eyes remained trained on Luke for a long second before he turned his attention to the book in his hand. Opening it, he pointed to a line and began to speak animatedly with Alex.

Taking a deep breath, Luke deflated having collected the slightly worn color game card into a full deck in his hands. At least Matt hadn't seen them.

Even though it hadn't been one of the options that Luke had provided, Alex slept on the trundle in Matt's room. They'd gotten into a philosophical discussion about soul matches and, eventually, Luke had taken Alex' stuff and dropped it just inside Matt's door with a short, "I'm going to sleep. I suggest you think about it, too."

So, yeah, he'd been jealous that Matt had stolen his friend for the night but not as jealous as he thought he'd be. Alex wasn't just Luke's; it felt like she was family, like how he could be mad at Matt for 'stealing' mom's attention but still know that she loved them both.

Morning came quickly and Luke found himself fighting with the coffeemaker a bit more than usual.

"Can I talk to you?" It was Matt's voice coming across the room from the kitchen door.

Luke ground his teeth together, more from frustration with the coffeemaker than his brother. "You already are," he bit it out, but he couldn't be blamed for that since he hadn't had his morning coffee yet.

Crossing the room, Matt leaned heavily against the countertop next to Luke and the demonic machine he was fighting with. "Have you... do you know...?" He let his head fall back and look at the ceiling. Taking a puff of breath, he turned and caught Luke's eye, "Do you have your colors?"

So, he had noticed.

Giving up on the coffeemaker, Luke turned and pulled the almond milk from the fridge, pouring that into his mug instead of his usual morning beverage. He took a swig and put it down. "It's complicated."

Luke had expected Matt to go nuts. He had expected questions upon questions, screeching and yelling. He'd expected the sort of noises that came from his brother when people got their colors in his favorite movies and television shows.

That wasn't what happened, though. What happened shocked him even more.

"It's Casper, right?"

The almond milk almost got spewed across the room. Luke choked a little, "What?"

Matt smirked. "That was just as telling as an actual answer." He took the carton of almond milk and poured himself a glass. "Why haven't you said anything? I mean, I really like Casper. He's calm and considerate and really smart and-"

"Matt, he didn't get his colors."

Silence.

"What do you mean?" Matt put his cup back on the counter.

"I mean, it's complicated. I don't even have all of my colors. And..." Luke pointed a finger at his brother's open

71

mouth, knowing he was about to demand more answers, "I really can't have this conversation right now. I have to deal with Alex and Bella and Casper all day today. I promise, we can have this conversation tomorrow, deal?" He turned his determined expression into a pleading one.

Matt nodded. "I guess." The doorbell rang, and, without missing a beat, Matt raised an eyebrow, "And that'll be Casper now."

Rolling his eyes, Luke went to open the door. He tried to smother the blush that was creeping up his neck and toward his cheeks. Stupid Matt.

A peek through the peephole confirmed his brother's suspicion and Luke took a deep breath, steadying himself, before opening the door. "Hey, Casper."

"Hello, Luke. Is Alex up?"

Luke was going to answer 'no', but thumping noises rang out from the direction of Matt's room and then down the stairs. He turned to see Alex standing half-way down the stairs with bed-head and rumpled sleep clothes.

She rubbed at her eye. "I'm up." She yawned, big and comically. "Totally up."

Casper chuckled and his lips quirked up at one end. "I can tell, and you're completely ready to help my sister who's been freaking out for the last three hours about making sure the house is clean enough for guests."

Shoulders jerking and her expression scrunching up, Alex licked her bottom lip. "Give me twenty minutes and I'll be ready." With that, she turned and bounded back up the stairs.

Smiling, Luke couldn't believe how normal, how domestic, it all felt. It was so natural and a fun kind of mundane. He turned to Casper.

Matt stepped out of the kitchen and smiled generously. "Hi, Casper." He crossed the room, holding out a cup of cashew milk. "I know you prefer almond, but this is usually what you drink when you're at our house."

Taking the glass, Casper nodded. "Thank you. I don't usually have the opportunity to drink milk outside of my house. When I can, I try to make the most of it." He took a sip.

"Casper, I have a question."

Luke's insides froze. This was it. Matt was going to out him. Matt was going to make some comment or some really specific question and Casper would figure it out. Casper was so smart. In fact, all of these people were smart. How did Luke end up in the midst of all these geniuses?

"What is it?"

Luke felt like he was melting. He was a puddle, now.

"How do you feel about Alex?"

Casper looked at Matt head-on. They were almost the same height, which said a lot more about Matt's height than Casper's. Casper was about Luke's height, which was taller than most of the seniors; Matt was just freakishly tall and destined to be a giant. "She's nice and kind. She's great for Bella. She's probably the reason why Bella didn't fail when our father left; the rest of us did. Alex stepped up, became Bella's stability. I'm happy for them."

So Casper and Jordan must have both flunked.

Matt waved a hand around the air. "That's great Casper, really, but, I wanted to know how you felt about Alex. What is she to you? Did you know she was going to be your sister-in-law when you met her?"

Eyes widened in surprise but face still classically stoic, Casper thought about it for a moment. "I didn't explicitly know. It wasn't some voice in the back of my head telling me that she was going to marry my sister, but..." He donned a small smile. "I knew she was important, that she was someone that would be around for a long time." He turned to Luke, "You saw how I was when you first met me; I'm not very approachable and I don't make friends easily. I never have."

Luke was still staring at Casper and Casper was still staring at Luke when Matt spoke up. "So, it was easy to become her friend. Like it felt natural?"

Like a sigh, Casper nodded, still looking at Luke. "Natural sums it up pretty well." He pulled his eyes away to look at Matt.

The blush that Luke had caught in his neck earlier forced through the roadblock and crawled onto his face.

Luckily, Casper was paying attention to Matt instead of Luke. "She felt like extended family right from the start."

Chapter 7:

Casper's Perspective

He'd just graduated. Capers stared at his cap and gown, now retired, where they hung a white hanger hooked on the back of his door. This was crazy. He was done with high school, admittedly a year later than normal, but still.

Excited. That's what he felt. He was excited to be done, to be moving on to other things, bigger things.

He spun on his heel, following the light feeling in his chest to his window.

The grey sky was bright and the grey grass was twitching in the beginnings of a summer breeze.

But it was still grey.

"Well, that didn't last long," he mumbled, slouching against one side of his window seat. He pulled a foot up onto the seat cushion and wrapped his arms around the bent knee. Plopping his cheek onto the knee, he watched Luke's house out the window.

It was weird and amazing to be this close to finding your color match, but he wasn't sure what he had to do.

When he'd met Luke, he'd known it was something special. He'd known that Luke was going to be a big part of his life for a long time just like he'd known when he met Alex. And, honestly, he'd been extremely excited.

And Casper had made it his mission to get close to Luke, to meet everyone associated with Luke.

For a while, Casper thought that his color match was going to be Luke's brother, Matt. It made sense. Luke always spoke about how Casper reminded him of Matt or that they'd make great friends. But, when Casper finally met Matt, no colors bled into his vision. It wasn't special, not in the least.

Okay, that might be a bit of a lie. Matt had that same feeling about him that Luke did, that 'this person is going to be in your life for a long time and you might as well make friends with them now' feeling that Alex had come with.

And now...

Now, Casper was just confused. Luke had already said that he didn't have any other family, at least not that he knew of, and that left Casper really confused.

And if that weren't bad enough, Casper felt bad sometimes. It was like he was using Luke to try and find his color match. But that wasn't it anymore! Promise!

It had started out that way, but at this point, Luke was his best friend. The best friend he'd ever had, closer than even Bella at times. Which made this so hard because he really needed to talk to someone about this, and he didn't want to pester Bella with his overgrown moping.

There was a knock on the door, and, of course, it was Bella. "Hey, Casper, Alex texted me that she's on her way over. You want to text Luke that we're about ready to go for celebratory milkshakes?" She grinned.

Frozen in place, Casper just stared. Was this a sign that he should talk to her about it? Color matches were proof of some sort of fate, right? Maybe this was part of that fate.

She quirked her head to the side. "What's wrong?" She crossed the room and perched on the other side of the window seat. It was cramped; they hadn't both sat on it since they were little, well, since before Alex had come into their lives.

Casper looked out the window to gather his thoughts.

"Is it about Luke?"

Jerking his head back around, Casper almost connected his nose and his knee. To avoid other close calls, he dropped his leg down to the cushion. "What do you mean? About Luke?" He was weary of where this would go. He hadn't broached this subject with Bella before, not completely; he'd skimmed around it when he'd told Bella that he wasn't going with her and Alex to college.

That had been one hell of a conversation; perhaps, argument was a better term for it. Casper had received the scholarship from the Grey Foundation for the Medical Sciences, but by then, he had decided to stay near Luke. He'd tried to gloss over that by making it about letting Bella and Alex have space and by saying that he was tired of third-wheeling. He'd made sure never to name Luke. It was weird, but Luke was the first real friend he'd made since their father left. The only person he trusted outside of Bella and Alex. He didn't want to lose him, and putting entire states between them seemed to be counterintuitive, especially since Luke hated flying.

But now that Bella had brought this – whatever it is – up, Casper had to know. If it was something about Luke, he needed to know it. He needed to defend Luke if it was bad; he needed to congratulate Luke if it was good. He needed...

He needed to know what was happening. All of the lectures and professors and psycolorgists that they'd been to in the last year (and a few that Casper had taken the liberty to email questions to) hadn't been able to provide any answers.

"Oh, I thought Alex told you?" Bella said it light and airy; the way she usually spoke about Alex.

And in that instance, it rubbed Casper the exact wrong way. "Why would she tell me anything? She's your color match," he jabbed a finger at his sister to emphasize his point, "Your girlfriend," jab, "Your best friend." He pulled his hand back and crossed it over the other on his chest. "You two keep secrets from me all the time."

Bella jerked back, pressing against the opposite wall of the window seat with an expression somewhere between shock and horror and pity pinching at her face. "We don't mean to."

Deflating, Casper tossed his head back against the wall, staring at the ceiling. "I know you don't mean to." He followed a hairline crack in the ceiling with his eyes. "It's just that you were my friend and Alex took you away and now she's taking Luke away and I don't like it."

"Are you mad at Alex?!" Bella's temper flared up, just like it did whenever someone said anything bad about Alex. Luckily, Casper had expected it and waited until she got passed it on her own. Bella took a breath, "Sorry. You're frustrated with Alex, with the situation really."

Casper shrugged and lolled his head back to the window. Down below, Alex had arrived on her bike. She parked it out front of their house, out of Casper's view from his window, before skipping over to Luke's house to collect him.

Alex was very gay and Casper shouldn't be jealous, especially since Luke wasn't his color match. He was just his best friend.

One day, Luke would meet his color match and leave him, just like Bella.

"No, he won't."

He jerked at the voiced response to his thoughts; he must've been thinking aloud.

Bella reached a hand across and laid it on Casper's arm. "He really cares about you, about all of us." She scoffed a little. "Do you really think he would have been in that horrible skit if he didn't?"

Thinking back to the Spring Fling, Casper couldn't help but chuckle. They had re-enacted some famous color matches and explained some of the lectures they'd been to. Luke had been paired with Jesse in the skit, and Jesse had a way of going over the top. There may have been a sock-puppet involved, and yet Luke had powered through the rehearsals and performances without batting an eye.

Bella smiled, probably thinking about the same sort of things. "I can't believe we got 8 people to join! Our club didn't die." It was her turn to look out the window glassy-eyed.

Sighing, Casper couldn't tell her, but those 8 people were probably more a product of either their table or Matt's persuasion. Casper never wanted to be on the receiving end of Matt's cunning; he almost signed himself up again. The kid would make an excellent lawyer if he continued on that route.

"What's it feel like when you're around Alex?" Bella was still looking outside.

Casper followed her gaze down to where Alex was leading Luke over to their house. She was explaining something, probably about planes or robotics from their other club. Her arms were moving furiously around the air. Luke said something and she turned and started to explain with more vigor, stopping them in the grass between their houses.

Turning his gaze to his sister, Casper cataloged the softness in her features, the way a small smile had crept onto her face, her relaxed eyebrows. Letting out a breath he'd been holding, Casper knew this was it. This was when his ramshackle lie would fall apart. "Like that," he said simply.

Eyes flicking to him, Bella gave a curt nod. "So, do you think he's Jordan's color match?"

"What?!" Everything in Casper clenched and not in a good way. He felt sick. "Why would-?"

Lifting a hand in a nonchalant gesture, Bella relaxed back against the wall and closed her eyes, completely oblivious to Casper's pain. "I mean, he's not your color match, so that leaves Jordan."

Casper pressed a hand to his stomach. He was going to throw up. He was literally going to throw up. He jumped up and ran to the bathroom. Absently, he could hear Bella running after him, but he didn't actively think about it until he was retching into the toilet.

Patting his shoulder, Bella kept apologizing.

Once Casper was done, he slumped into a kneeling position in front of the toilet, absolutely exhausted. He closed his eyes and tried to get his breathing back. He wiped at his forehead where he'd broken a sweat and took the warm washcloth that Bella offered, continuing to clean his face and mouth.

She flushed the toilet for him.

With the adrenaline fading, Casper realized just how messed up all of this was, how telling his reaction was.

Bella sat on the edge of the tub. "So, do you like him?" Her voice was wary like she wasn't sure if the words would set him off again.

"I don't know, Bella." Casper rubbed the heels of his hands into his eyes. "I don't think so. He's my best friend; I just don't want to lose him." Anger bubbled up inside of

Casper's chest. "Especially not to Jordan." Casper turned to the floor, muttering, "Fuck, Jordan."

When he turned back to Bella, she had her elbow on her knee and her head in her hand, looking at him with an unreadable expression, the sort of look she'd use when she was doing an experiment in their AP Biology class.

He wasn't some science experiment. He turned away and let the silence eat at the walls.

Bella looked up when footfalls sounded from the stairs. The steps got closer, pausing twice – probably at each of their rooms – on the way to the bathroom.

A gasp sounded from the doorway. "Casper! Are you pregnant?"

Turning slowly, Casper knew his face was pinched into something irritated and confused. When he saw Alex, there was an exaggeratedly shocked expression, her hands on each cheek and her mouth open; he threw her the finger.

His gaze shifted to Luke who was standing over Alex's shoulder with a more believable look of concern. "Are you okay?"

"I just threw up. I'm not dying," Casper deadpanned in his usual way of deflecting emotions; he didn't want to have to give the whole explanation to Luke. Instead, he shifted his attention, watching as Alex and his sister had a silent conversation over his head.

Bella turned a wobbly smile toward Casper, "So, I think we're going to skip milkshakes today."

Shaking his head, Casper began to stand up. He didn't get far. He closed the toilet seat lid and sat there. "You guys can still go. I'll go another time." He turned to see what he already knew was there, Alex's grateful expression.

She winked and pointed at him. "You're the best, Casper! Come on, Bella." And with Alex dragging Bella by the elbow, they exited the bathroom and left down the stairs.

"You're going to miss the celebratory milkshakes," Casper said to the wall, not wanting to look at Luke.

Luke leaned against the bathroom counter; Casper could tell by the creaking noise that followed. Luke huffed, "We can go another day. Besides, there's no room on the bike for me." He chuckled at his own joke, probably an attempt to lighten the mood.

Stubborn and holding onto the bad mood he'd surrounded himself in, Casper turned to Luke. "I'm sorry for getting sick on graduation day."

Luke looked good standing there, like he belonged. Casper wasn't sure what he'd do when Luke found his color match. It wasn't something he wanted to think about, especially with what Bella had pointed out. He just wanted to keep his best friend. His best friend that felt like family, who might even be Jordan's color match.

Thinking about it, Casper realized that it might be possible. Luke and Jordan had the same sort of humor and both liked sweets. Luke and Jordan both had an affinity for old cars and practical jokes. Luke and Jordan hadn't met yet. Maybe, when Jordan came back after his trip with his friends, he and Luke would look at each other and get their colors and leave him behind, leave him grey and alone.

No matter how much Casper hated to admit it, Jordan wasn't a bad person. Maybe he could be happy with Luke as a brother-in-law. At least, Luke couldn't completely leave him. They'd be family, real family.

Luke held out a hand to Casper, offering to help him up. "How about we go downstairs and watch all of the new Star Trek movies back-to-back?"

Taking the proffered hand, Casper nodded. Yeah, maybe he could get used to brother-in-law Luke.

Chapter 8:

The Mandatory Beach Episode

(because every anime needs some fanservice)

Luke was impressed how well Matt got along with everyone. Upon second thought, he realized that it shouldn't have been a surprise. Matt was smart and mature for his age, much like Alex, and he had an interest in color matches, which was the whole reason the rest of them hung out together.

Through an infuriating group message, the GCA had managed to put together a beach day. They had packed sandwiches for lunch and brought packets of hotdogs and buns for dinner.

Walking back up the beach after getting tagged in a weird game that Bella and Casper had made up when they were little - something between tag and dodgeball in the water -

Luke joined Jesse under the umbrella that Billy had gotten for discount from his boss.

Jesse looked scrawny in his t-shirt and jeans, but, somehow, he managed to look scrawnier in swim trunks and huge sunglasses. He was reclined into a makeshift lounger dug into the sand and covered with the towels.

"Enjoying your nap?" Luke deposited himself into the other side of the towel-covered ditch. It was comfier than it looked.

Jesse lazily turned his head. "I'm not asleep. I'm just contemplating."

One of Luke's eyebrows rose, he could feel the tell-tale tightness from being in the sun too long. "Contemplating what?" He reached for the sunscreen near Bella's bag and began to reapply, wondering if he should remind the others.

"The finer things." Jesse grabbed a water from the cooler and twisted it open.

"So, that didn't actually tell me anything about what you were thinking about."

"Color matches." Jesse recapped the bottle and placed it next to him. "I was thinking about color matches."

Luke hadn't thought much about Jesse and his colors and color match situation. Jesse always seemed so happy and optimistic that Luke never considered that he was unhappy. "Anything in particular?"

Shrugging, Jesse pulled his sunglasses from his head. "Just, what if I never find her? I mean, what if I walk right by her?"

"That won't happen. She'll get her colors and chase after you." Luke held the sunscreen bottle out to him. "Could you get my back?"

Jesse nodded and took the bottle, somewhat absentminded. "But what if I get away? Maybe we pass each other and I'm getting on a plane or onto a train, and she doesn't get to me in time?" He smoothed some sunscreen onto Luke's back.

Wincing at the temperature of the cream, Luke tried not to think of earlier when Casper had helped him do this. He'd probably been really red and breathing weird. It had felt intimate. Despite him and Jesse doing the exact same thing only a little while later, it wasn't the same. It was intimate but solely platonic.

Luke recovered his voice, "That's oddly specific. I wouldn't worry too much about it. Soulmates are something cosmic; I'm sure it'll work out."

Jesse's hands disappeared from his back.

Turning around, Luke saw Jesse looking for something to wipe his hands on. He managed to grab a sandless towel from the stack and toss it into Jesse's lap before he wiped the sunscreen off onto his swim trunks.

Wiping his hands, Jesse threw an unsure smile in Luke's direction. "Casper said about the same thing. I'm sure you guys are right."

A brand-new flush threatened to spread across Luke's face and upper torso. If anyone asked, he'd blame the sun. Luke busied himself with drawing lines in the sand with a stick.

"How's that going, by the way?"

"How's what going?"

"You and Casper and your colors?"

Luke almost broke the stick. He whipped his head around to see if anyone was close enough to have heard what

Jesse said. When no one was, he turned to Jesse. "How do you know about that?"

Holding his hands up in mock-surrender, Jesse hastened to reply, "Billy told me. He didn't mean to tell me, but he thought I was Alex and mentioned something. I've been sworn to secrecy, lips locked, key forgotten, and all that."

Grinding his teeth, Luke flashed a glare at Billy.

Billy was still playing the water-dodgeball-tag game, but froze and stared back at Luke when he noticed. He seemed to figure out what had happened and offered a sheepish smile and a shrug.

"It really was an accident. It's just the four of us that know, Billy, Alex, me, and you."

"And Matt," Luke added, annoyed with the turn of events. Basically, everyone knew. Why can't people keep secrets?

Jesse pointed around at people, counting them off silently. "So, everyone but the Miltons know?"

Luke pulled his knees to his chest and buried his face there. "Unless you count Alex as a Myer."

"True."

They lapsed into silence. The sound of the others splashing around in the water seemed deafening despite the absence of walls.

"At least you know who your soulmate is supposed to be." Jesse's voice was tiny and almost lost behind the noises of the game.

Luke lifted his head. "At least you have all your colors."

They nodded at each other in co-misery. After the moment passed, Luke lifted his chin to his knees and looked out at the others.

Alex was soaked from head to toe; her hair plastered to her neck and shoulders. In contrast, Bella was unscathed, practically dry from the waist up. Luke was trying to figure out how she'd managed that until Matt threw the ball making a huge splash in their direction. Alex jumped in front of Bella, taking the brunt of the spray.

The next person to get ahold of the ball was Billy, and, when he did, he sent it hurtling at Matt who had to dive into the water to get away. Unfortunately, Matt got tagged with the ball, so he was officially out. When Matt surfaced, he and Alex began to argue over whether he was really out or not. Oh well.

Luke's gaze panned over to Casper. He wasn't even paying attention to the others or the game. He was looking in Luke's general direction, eyes further away than they should be.

Shifting into Casper's line of sight, Luke offered a short wave.

Casper jerked and turned away, probably embarrassed from zoning out.

One day, Casper would fly back from college, take one look at him and get his colors. Hopefully. Luke still hadn't found any scientific evidence to support that, so it was just an educated guess.

Luke leaned back, unfolding his knees and bracing himself on his hands. He crossed his fingers. Hopefully, one day Casper would be his. All his. And honestly, Luke had never really thought of himself as a selfish guy. He was pretty good at sharing his things, but Casper seemed to be different. It was like Luke wanted to keep him in his pocket wherever he went, wanted Casper to bottle up everything he did when Luke wasn't around and gift it to him when he saw him again, just to make sure that Luke didn't miss anything that was inherently Casper-like. He wanted him all to himself. Casper, with his tan body and broad shoulders, with his strange, paisley-print trunks, with his bright blue eyes, with his gummy smile, with his- Shit. He was coming this way.

"Anything interesting going on up here?" Casper unfolded another towel and sat outside the umbrella's shade on the other side of Luke.

Jesse groaned from where he'd relaxed into his sand-lounge. "Just a pleasant nap that you've interrupted." He huffed and grew still again, apparently intent on resuming.

Luke sat back up, sitting up and turning to Casper. "Did you lose the game?"

Blushing a little, Casper stared down at where he began to draw designs in the sand with his index finger. "No." He flicked his eyes back to Luke. He seemed a little embarrassed, maybe?

"What is it?" Luke leaned forward into Casper's space. "What don't you want to tell me?" He had donned a playful smirk, knowing that Casper would just ignore him and not tell him if he really didn't want to.

Casper rolled his eyes and pointed a look back out where the others were playing in the water, well, arguing really.

95

"Your brother is very competitive." He turned back to Luke.

Shrugging, Luke ignored Casper's gaze and watched his brother fling the ball at Billy. "We moved around a lot. You either had to get competitive or you had to become passive. It's just the way he went." Luke pushed up to his knees. "I'll go calm him down, remind him it's just a game." He went to get up but was stopped by a hand on his wrist.

When Luke turned back, Casper had a deep red scorching the tips of his ears and his eyes trained out on the water. "Don't."

Luke sagged back down so he was sitting on his towel again. He didn't pry his wrist from Casper's grip, instead placing it near enough to Casper that he wouldn't have to let go. Luke really didn't want him to let go. He just kept staring at where they were touching.

"It's nice to see Alex act her age." Casper wore a soft smile.

They lapsed into silence. Luke wondered if Jesse had actually fallen asleep, but, when Luke glanced in his direction, he was met with a lewd smirk and a waggling eyebrow above his shades. Luke jerked back to looking at the waves, suddenly fighting a monumental flush.

The game broke up after Matt and Alex got into another argument. It wasn't a bad argument, just that they were both too competitive for their own good. Honestly, Luke should have seen it coming.

With the game over, Billy trudged back up toward them. "It should be about time for us to reapply sunscreen." He pulled out his spray can and gently kicked Jesse's side asking for his help. "Spray me."

Jesse begrudgingly got up to help Billy and Bella stole his spot in the trench under the umbrella. As if she were trained, Alex came and sat directly in front of her, baring her back to get lathered with sunscreen. Alex's fair skin needed more protection than the spray sunscreens offered, so Bella had to apply the SPF 150 by hand. Alex didn't seem to mind.

Luke tended to have the same problem with sunscreen as Alex; he wasn't a red-head, but he had a fairer complexion that bred freckles and sun damage.

"I can help you, again?" Casper snatched the SPF 150 bottle from around Luke's back, his skin brushing against Luke's and causing all kinds of reactions in Luke's body, mainly butterflies.

Fully intent on telling Casper that he'd already reapplied, Luke spun around to his friend. But instead of explaining the situation, Luke found himself in a new one, nose-to-nose with Casper. Luke held his breath. What was he supposed to do? Why did this happen to him?

Casper turned away first, thank God.

And Luke could breathe again, air rushing into his lungs. He tried to control his breathing so he didn't look so obviously affected.

Hearing the tell-tale sound of sunscreen being squeezed into a hand, Luke simply ran with it. What could too much sunscreen do? He turned a little so that Casper could reach his back, sure that his face was bright red.

Luckily, Bella was too busy attending to Alex to notice Luke's blush or Billy's wink or Jesse's thumbs-up. Seriously, could they tone it down?

Staring at the ground, Luke tried not to think about the hands on his back, but they were really nice. Big and smooth and, honestly, Luke felt like sand, falling away with every movement of those fingers. Luke felt his ears heat up when Casper's hands trailed up to his neck. Casper hadn't done that last time; Luke had applied sunscreen to his own neck.

Oh, but it felt good. Luke bit his lip and closed his eyes. What was he? A desperate character in a soap opera?

Billy finished spraying Matt, which was nice of him because Luke was obviously indisposed.

"You need to do your front, Luke." Casper poked at Luke's arm before going back to his task.

Letting out a breathy laugh and hoping it didn't sound too out-of-place, Luke shrugged a little and stirred up some bravado in his chest, using it to disguise his flustered state. "Figured I'd wait until either you or Bella was done. Didn't need to have three people fighting over the bottle."

Bella was taking her time on Alex. She was moving her hands in smooth, confident strokes. She turned and offered Luke a small grin. "It's okay. Go ahead and get some; I'm on the last bit anyway." Alex made a small noise in her throat as some sort of protest.

"We're gonna start up the barbecue for dinner. Sound good?" Jesse hooked his thumbs over his shoulders toward one of the public barbecues.

There was a murmur of agreement.

Shooting his hand up in the air, Matt exclaimed, "I want to help," which brought on a few snickers, too.

Jesse grinned. "Okay. Let's get going."

Groaning, Billy uncrossed his arms from over his chest. Resigned, he mumbled, "I'm gonna go supervise. Y'all good here?"

"Yes." Casper's curt answer was a bit closer to Luke's ear than he'd expected and he jumped little in response. Casper's hands kneaded into Luke's back, pulling a yelp from Luke's mouth. "We're good here."

Luke caught Alex's eyes. She was watching Casper over Luke's shoulder. Her face was tugged into an expression between confused, skeptical, and surprised, and, honestly, Luke didn't want to worry about it at that moment.

The sun was beating down; the air was cooling off. Casper's hands were on Luke, and, for a brief moment, Luke could pretend that they could both see the rolling blues of the waves.

Chapter 9:

Extended Family

Luke hefted a box into his arms, looking around Bella's room. This was it. This was the end. Why was it over so soon? He'd only moved in next door a year ago – wow, a year ago – and it was already time to say goodbye.

He looked out the window to the ground below. Alex's new-to-her, yellow Gremlin was sitting in the driveway with the back hatch open.

Casper, Bella, and Alex were leaving.

Sighing, Luke turned toward the door to make his way out with the box.

They were all going off to college. They were all leaving Luke.

But, that could be good. Or, at least he kept telling himself that. This is just the first step toward Casper getting his colors, right?

Luke still hadn't been able to get any academically verifiable proof that his theory was even plausible. There was a huge chance that he was just broken. Huge. Casper could go off to college and meet some girl who gives him his colors. What would that mean for Luke?

But, he wasn't going to think about that. If he thought about it too much, he'd trip down the remainder of the staircase with a box of possibly fragile things that belonged to Bella. Shaking his head, he shifted the box in his arms trying to figure out which step was the last step.

Alex came through the open door and waited for him to finish getting down the stairs before racing up them herself. "We're on the last ones, Luke! Isn't this exciting?"

Her excitement was almost palpable while Luke's was nonexistent. He plastered a small smile on his face, trying to be as encouraging as possible in his current state.

"I need to get my towels," Bella groaned.

"Why didn't you think about it before you packed them?"

"Because I didn't, okay?" Bella pulled the boxes out of the trunk, completely counterproductive to their goal. She placed them in two stacks at the back bumper. "Ah, this is the one." She balanced the box between her thighs and the car.

Putting the newest box down, Luke took a break from the packing, wiping the sweat from his forehead onto his jeans and crossing his arms over his chest. He was trying to memorize everyone.

It wasn't just Casper that was leaving. It was all of them were leaving. They'd become Luke's life, his family. Luke had his mother and his brother, but Casper and Bella and Alex were just as important. It was the family he'd found. He'd managed to situate himself into their lives in such a way that it was perfectly domestic.

He was losing his best confidant and his best friend ever and... well, Bella was something special too but Luke didn't have a word for it.

"Are you nervous about going? You don't usually overlook these sorts of things." Casper used a key from his key chain to cut the box open. He was looking at Bella with a concerned expression, wrinkles appearing the top of his nose from his eyebrows squeezing together.

"I'll get some tape to shut the box again." Anything to get out of hefting another box quite yet. Luke spun around to go back into the house.

With his back turned, his smile fell again. What was wrong with him? He should be excited for them. He should be out there encouraging Bella. Instead, he was inside the house being selfish and looking through the kitchen, looking for the patented junk drawer. No matter how immaculate the Miltons' house was, they couldn't be above having a junk drawer.

Apparently they could.

So, Luke started up the stairs hoping that between Casper's and Bella's packing there would be a roll of tape upstairs.

"I got it."

Looking up, Luke had to freeze between the third and fourth steps because Bella was coming down, holding a roll of packing tape in one of her hands. "Oh, sorry. I went looking in the kitchen." He quirked a brow and let a smirk creep onto his face. "You know, normal families keep this sort of shit in a junk drawer in the kitchen."

Bella waved the tape around in a nonchalant circle, before leveling her eyes with Luke and stating in a matter-of-fact tone, "Well excuse us. We keep our junk drawer in the study." She slid past him and out the door. "But you're not allowed in there." She shrugged as she joked at Luke.

She was like an older sister that Luke had never had or really wanted. Of course, he only realized that when she was about to leave. God, he was an idiot.

It probably wouldn't be so hard if he didn't have his colors. It probably wouldn't have turned out so difficult if he hadn't let himself think of them as his long-lost family. He'd gotten used to the idea that Casper was his color match, that Alex and Bella would be his sisters-in-law... sister-in-laws?? Whatever.

He was just too naïve. How could he let himself get so relaxed about something so critical? Fuck.

Alex and Bella were at the car when Luke returned. Bella was scolding Alex for doing such an ugly job of retaping the box shut.

"Well, if it annoys you so much, you could just tape it again." Alex shrugged and held the tape out to Bella.

When Luke caught sight of the box, he almost laughed. He ended up covering it with a cough since Bella was glaring at him. The tape spelled out 'idiot' across the box's seam.

Huffing at the both of them, Bella turned and stomped up to the driver's seat and got to work fiddling with the CDs and USB cords.

Luke and Alex put the boxes back into the car. Alex was having a field day. She was humming some Tetris-sounding tune and kept making a popping sound when they filled a line with boxes, even though the lines were more like bingo than like Tetris.

Stepping back, Alex wiped the back of her hand across her forehead. "Well, looks like we've got just enough room for the last box." She smiled brightly.

Come to think of it, Luke was struck with a question. "How will Casper get his stuff in there? Are you guys heading out early for a honeymoon or something?" He tried to make his tone teasing, especially with the last question, because he didn't want them to know just how many emotions were attacking him. If Casper was sticking around a bit longer, Luke could make a better goodbye. It would also just delay the inevitable and make it super awkward because it would just be the two of them and-

Casper emerged from the house and strode to the car. Luke stepped forward toward Alex to make room for him

to put the box into the perfectly-sized slot they'd left in the trunk.

Returning from the front of the car, Bella stood next to Alex, comfortably close. It was so nice that the two of them were so comfortable with each other that they basically could stand there as a single unit. Bella flicked her eyes from Alex to Luke to somewhere behind Luke, presumably Casper. "Casper, you didn't tell him?"

"Tell him what?" Alex's voice was still as excited and anxious as it had been all day, but suddenly a little trickle of skepticism had been present. She turned herself entirely toward her girlfriend. "What didn't you tell me?" She looked shocked.

Whispering, Bella turned Alex away from the boys, seeming to want a private conversation.

Luke could grant them that. He turned around to try to accommodate and was caught off-guard by a red-faced Casper.

He was biting his lip and flicking his eyes to look anywhere but at Luke. "I turned down my acceptance to the University of Washington." He still wouldn't look at Luke.

"But why?" Was something wrong? What had happened? Casper had been over the moon with the news when his acceptance letter had come in the mail. He'd gone on and on for well over a week. It couldn't be the money; was their mother sick or something? "You got the fancy grey scholarship and you were looking forward to going there. Why would you change your mind?" Luke's mouth was hanging open, but he couldn't seem to summon enough energy to close it, instead using the little energy he could muster to flick his eyes over Casper's face looking for some sign.

Casper shrugged and stared over Luke's shoulder. "The scholarship money goes a lot further at a cheaper university, you know?"

That sentence didn't sound much like Casper. It was much too ambiguous? Uncertain? Casper made every decision with purpose and a list of calculated risks. What was so important to Casper that he was giving up on his top-choice university?

What was so secretive that he didn't want to tell Luke?

Luke felt small, like he was a toddler and Casper was a grown up telling him that he'd explain it when Luke was older. He wanted to know now, but he also didn't want to touch the subject since it was obviously a rough spot. Directing his gaze downward, Luke resigned himself to not knowing. "Um, okay. So, uh, where are you going?" He sucked in a big breath, feeling like he wasn't getting enough air in his lungs to continue this conversation. The bigger question came next. "When are you leaving?"

"I'm not?"

Blink. Luke slowly looked up to find Casper pointedly looking up at the sky. His face was still pink, probably not fully recovered from the full red-face he'd had only a minute before. "You're not?"

It was Bella's voice from behind him that spoke next. "He's decided to go to KU."

But, that was where Luke was going. They were going to college together? Awesome! Wait. Not awesome. Casper was supposed to go off to college, get away from Luke, then come back and suddenly get his colors. How would that work if he wasn't leaving? This was a disaster.

But, if it was a disaster, why did Luke feel so happy?

Because he's lonely and selfish; that's why.

"I can always transfer to another university after two years or use the extra money to study abroad. Besides, it's the medical school that really matters; I could get the preparatory degree anywhere. Heck, maybe I end up at Johns Hopkins or–"

Bella paced around Luke and put a hand on her brother's shoulder. "You're rambling." She was grinning when she turned to Luke. "So, I guess you're gonna have to take care of him while we're gone."

Snickering, Alex grabbed Luke's upper arms and leaned over one of his shoulders. "You have to feed him at least twice a day and walk him every morning."

"I'm older than all of you." Casper turned away like a ruffled toddler. "I can take care of myself."

"It's okay." Luke smiled. "Extended family, right?"

The air became static and Luke could have sworn that his ears popped.

Alex's hands fell off of his arms as she retracted from him, like she was physically shocked by the electricity in the moment.

Standing there with his mouth agape and his eyes wide, Casper stared unblinkingly at Luke.

Colors.

All of the colors.

Luke could see the different flecks of blue in Casper' eyes. He could see the shifts in Casper's skin tone over the plane of his cheek. He could see the muted browns and blacks of his hair under the sun.

The world became defined by lowlights and highlights and tints and shades.

Bella had stepped away from Casper in much the same way as Alex had from Luke. She was watching with wide, glimmering eyes, glimmering with little flecks of happiness that had different colors that Luke could identify.

"Luke." Casper's voice was breath. It was light and ghostly and timid. "Your eyes are so green." He lifted a hand and touched Luke's face. "I mean, Bella told me they were green, but they're greener than that."

So, Luke tends to ruin moods. "That made no sense," he replied automatically; his brain was still rushing to catch up with everything that was going on.

With that response, Casper's hand began to fall from Luke's face. His awed expression dented by a little twitch in his eyelids and a quirk at his lips.

111

Shit. Shit. Luke scooped up Casper's hand and put it back on his face. He opened his mouth, but he still had nothing to say. This was shit. He'd been practicing this. He'd known this would happened; at least, he'd hoped it would. He needed to say something. Anything. "I didn't expect you to get your colors so soon."

Epilogue:

Red Wedding

It had been a wonderful ceremony. Alex had worn a white suit and Bella had worn a red dress. It was already out of the ordinary, so it didn't much matter that they broke tradition any further.

I mean, they had red solo cups on the tables at the reception.

"The Chinese wear red dresses at weddings to symbolize life and good luck." Matt took his seat at the table in front of his name card. He tucked the table cloth around him a little.

Luke rolled his eyes, taking the seat next to him and switching his and Casper' name plaques.

Glaring at where Luke had swapped their name cards, Casper lowered himself slowly to the chair, like he would set off an alarm if he didn't sit in his assigned spot. After throwing that glare in Luke's direction for a long moment, he turned to Matt with softened features. "In traditional Chinese weddings, yes, but many western traditions have been adopted there. White dresses for brides is one of them." He turned back and glared at his name card. "What if we were sitting in a specific spot for a reason?"

"What reason would there be?" Luke raised an eyebrow and waited.

Billy took a seat on the other side of Matt. "Food. The catering might bring you the wrong food." He pointed out.

"We ordered the same thing."

"You ordered the fish?" Casper turned a scowl at Luke. "You? The fish?"

The eyes of everyone who'd found their table were looking at him. They all knew that Luke liked red meat. Blushing a little, Luke fiddled with his place setting. "Yeah, so?"

Matt laughed. "I don't believe you. You couldn't have ordered the fish." He shook his head, his now shaggy hair flopping around. "There's just no way."

By then Tammy had found the table too. "So, what are we laughing about?" She took her seat on the far side of Casper. "And why aren't you up there?" She nodded toward the head table at the front of the room.

"I think my mother is punishing me." Casper shot a deadpan look at his mother.

Tammy paused where she'd been situating her legs under the table. "For what?"

"For marrying me." Luke glowered at the table. The embarrassment from the previous conversation eaten away by the guilt replacing it.

Under the table, Casper's hand found Luke's and offered a quick squeeze. "Not for marrying you," he said it soft almost into Luke's ear. He turned back to Tammy. "For not telling her."

"Well, any mother would be pissed about that." Billy grabbed a bread-stick-cracker-thing from a ribbon-wrapped red, Solo cup at the center of the table. "I would've been pissed about that."

Luke's brain briefly reminded him of when Billy had first found out that Luke had kept his colors secret. It was a good thing that Billy didn't know how long they'd kept their marriage secret.

None of them did.

The story went that Luke had convinced Casper to marry him as an early birthday present. Little did anyone know, they were actually married almost a year earlier. Sharon was mad because she didn't know about the supposed birthday one, and Luke and Casper were planning to keep the real one a secret for as long as possible.

If Sharon ever found out that they'd waited a year to tell her, Casper would probably be disowned.

Which reminded him...

"How's Jordan doing?" Luke turned to Casper.

Casper sent him a glare. "This is hardly the time or place to discuss that." He darted his eyes around. "We are surrounded by my extended, very conservative family. It's surprising no one has come over to passive-aggressively congratulate us yet."

Leaning in, Matt whispered, "What's up with Jordan?"

"He's been disowned." Luke whispered back.

When Casper squeezed Luke's hand again, it was a warning. He narrowed his eyes at the brothers.

"I'll tell you later," Luke managed to grit out as Casper' grip got tighter. When he finished, Casper' hand went slack in his, signaling his relief.

Since Jordan wasn't there and Casper wasn't at the head table, it was only occupied by Bella, Alex, and Sharon. Alex looked very uncomfortable. Bella didn't look uncomfortable, but her movements were stiff.

"Where's Jesse?" Matt looked around. "Isn't he beside you?" He craned over to look at the name plaque on the far side of Billy.

Billy shrugged. "He's supposed to be, but he got to talking with the girl in the row behind us. They're still yapping away." He motioned across the room.

Most of the guests had taken their seats by then, so it was very easy to see Jesse sitting next to a someone just as gangly as he was. He was leaning on a propped-up elbow, listening to her talk.

"Her friend was asking her what colors everything was. And it turns out that she randomly got her colors a few years back, so they're talking about that." Billy shrugged.

"Well, they were talking about that. They probably aren't anymore."

Luke nodded. He was going to say something, but was interrupted by a hand on his shoulder. He turned to that, mouth hanging slightly open.

"Hey!" Once she had his attention, Alex slid down further, giving Luke a hug over the back of his chair. "Guess what?"

Knowing where it was going, Luke smiled, "What?"

"I'm married!" She squeezed tight and Luke couldn't help but squeeze her arms where they were crossed over his chest.

They slid away from each other and he turned in his chair so he could speak more directly to her. "So, where did you guys decide to honeymoon?"

He and Casper hadn't gotten a honeymoon. They'd tied the knot just before Casper left to go to medical school. Luke had followed once he'd gotten his degree and found a new job, but they'd wanted to make it official before they parted ways.

Alex slumped over. "No honeymoon."

"What? Why not?" It came out almost as a whine. Luke hung an arm over the back of his chair and leaned his chin on his wrist.

"We're trying to pay off student loans first. Then we'll go party ourselves out in Mexico for two weeks." She leaned forward and whispered at Luke. "You and Casper and Jordan and Kali can come too. We can have an amazingly gay and 'absolutely humiliating' time." She used a mocking voice to quote Sharon from when she'd found out about Jordan and Kali. Kali was a stripper who also happened to be Jordan's color match. "I mean, your honeymoon is 2 years overdue."

3 years, actually. "Yeah. It could be fun." Since Casper had received the scholarship, he hardly had any debt. It was great. And yeah, they'd contacted The Grey Foundation to let them know that Casper had gotten his colors, but since all the paperwork had already gone through, it stuck. When they got the ClearColor glasses, they'd donated them to the GCA at their old school.

Bella slid into her usual place next to Alex. "So, how is it over here?"

Smiling a little, Casper looked up at his sister. "It's a lot less condescending."

They laughed, because, if they didn't, it would be sad.

"Congratulations, girls." Tammy smiled at them with a trace of pity evidenced by the slight quirk in her eyebrows. "I'm glad that your mother still took part."

Biting his lip, Luke tried not to feel like his mother was blaming him for not telling her about being married to Casper. Her pity was probably more about the dysfunction evident in the Myer family, but he couldn't help but feel chastised.

"Yeah." Bella offered a tight smile. "With everything that's happened, I think I'm the favorite child again."

Billy piped up, "How will you know who people are asking for on the phone? They'll be asking for Mrs. Myer-Smythe, right?" He was munching on another Italian breadstick.

"Easy," Alex leered at him, "I'm Mrs. And she's Dr."

Barking out a quick laugh, Matt excused himself from the table. "Going to find a restroom before the formalities start up again." He patted on Luke's shoulder to assure him it was nothing else.

Luke nodded to him.

"At this rate, he'll never make his way over here." Casper was looking over at Jesse, who had begun to explain something using his hands. The girl he was talking to was laughing and nodding along.

"Huh." Bella sunk into one of her hips. "I never would've guessed that Jesse and Lily would hit it off. I mean, Lily is very..." She thought for a moment before finishing her thought, "organized."

Everyone was thinking it, but Billy was the only one to voice it. "And Jesse is anything but."

Bella turned back to the table, "Also, despite what Alex said, we're not changing our names. At least not yet."

"Oh? Why not?" Casper tilted his head up to look at Alex.

Alex rolled her eyes. "We can't all be like you, Casper Batton." She emphasized his last name.

Shrugging, Casper reached out for Luke. "I like my last name."

"I figure that someday I'll take Alex's last name, just not today." Bella sighed. "Not when I'm on Mom's good side."

"Fair enough." Luke gave a curt nod.

Content silence settled for a long moment.

"So, who's that?" Billy nodded his head in Jesse's direction.

A young woman with blonde hair wearing a light green dress cut between Lily and Jesse to grab her name card from the table. She hurriedly tried to bow out, but was caught by Jesse speaking to her.

They couldn't hear what he was saying despite their eyes being trained on the scene.

The woman only left after Jesse pointed over at them. He didn't even really see them, turning back to keep looking at and talking to Lily instead.

She walked over timidly, waving a little at Alex and Bella. "Congratulations. I can't wait for work next week because everyone will be tripping over themselves with names. Get ready for that chaos." She offered a weak smile at Alex; she seemed nervous.

But why?

Luke felt like she was perfect.

And then it happened. A little more color bled into Luke's vision. Where Casper was holding his hand, he squeezed tighter; he must've had the same thing happen.

Alex leaned heavily on the back of Luke's chair and whispered into his ear. "This is Tess."

That wasn't a new name. Alex had told Luke about Tess. About how she thought she brought about a similar feeling to the one Luke had brought, that 'this person is very important' feeling.

Before Luke could react, Tammy popped up from her seat, offering a hand. "Hi, I'm Tammy Batton. I'm guessing that you'll be taking Jesse's place at our table since he stole yours." She nodded to where Jesse had scooted his chair into the table on the other side of the room.

Tammy must've felt it too.

Tess flushed a pretty shade of pink. "Yeah, that's, uh, that's exactly what happened."

Clearing his throat, Luke shot up from his chair, earning him a grunt from Alex who was thrown off balance and Casper who had to let go of his hand. Luke swung his hand forward to match his mom's greeting. "And I'm Luke and this is my partner, Casper." He motioned to Casper.

"Hello." She smiled. "So, how do you all know Bella and Alex?" She gingerly took her seat next to Billy, covering Jesse's name card with her own.

Alex popped her head out from behind Luke. "Casper is Bella's brother." She offered a huge smile full of too-white teeth. Almost laughing, Luke remembered that conversation very well; she'd insisted on getting them whitened for the wedding citing that if she was going to wear a white suit, her teeth could not be yellow.

Pausing with her fidgets, Tess took a sweeping look over everyone. "So, you're all related?"

"Not me." Billy leaned back in his chair. "I am not part of that weird family."

Bella pointed a finger at him. "Well, you might as well be. You've known Casper and Jesse and I longer than Alex has." She tutted at him.

All Billy did was shrug, looking smug about not actually being related to them.

They were all talking by then, but Alex tugged on Luke's wrist, pulling his ear to her. "She'll be part of this crazy family soon enough." She giggled.

Her giddiness was infectious. Luke couldn't wait. Matt had been waiting for his soul match forever.

Matt walked back up to the table, coming from the far door. He couldn't see Tess' face yet. Everyone was basically sitting at the edge of their seat, dying from their anxiousness. He looked around at them all. "Why are you all looking at me like that? Did I miss something important?"

Laughing nervously, Tess snorted, "Not unless I'm important." She stood from her chair. "I'm Tess. I was kicked out of my table by your friend, Jesse. It's a pleas-" She finally turned to him.

For a split second, Luke was worried that they'd have the same issues that Luke and Casper had, but, by the way both Matt's and Tess' eyes widened, his worry melted away.

Alex hopped up with a huge grin. "Now, you're part of the family, too!"

Through the celebratory cheers and happiness, Luke could hear Billy groan, "No. No more," before reluctantly joining in.

Author's Note

Hello everyone! I hope you enjoyed this fic as much as I do!

I originally wrote this for the Asexual Supernatural Mini Bang project and it is still available as fanfiction online on my Archive of Our Own account, TheAuthorGod, along with 50+ other Supernatural fanfictions.

A bit about myself, I am an agender individual, hence the penname MxKnowitall, who identifies as asexual and panromantic. I am a Mathematician by education and a teacher by experience.

Some of my other creative endeavors include fanfiction, fanart, original writing and art, card games, and role play games. I started writing original content at the prime age of three and started publishing my work informally at 13 and formally at 16.

If you liked this book, please review it on Amazon or let me know on another site like Facebook, Tumblr, Archive of Our Own, or Instagram!

A Peek

into MxKnowitall's full-length,

coming-of-age novel,

Spork

Scene 1

Life tries to throw curve balls. I like to think that I can
catch them in my catcher's mitt, woven with sarcasm and
'don't give a fuck'; but not all curve balls can be caught.
Some can merely be avoided or barely missed. Sometimes,
they hit you square in the gut and you have to be grateful
that you're wearing a bulletproof vest made of bits of pain
and your personal history.

But life just throws another.

Like a text message that I received that morning.

> R, did you see the post?

I replied:

> What post?

His response:

> THE post.

I wasn't sure what he meant. I really had no care for the
posts of the opinions and misguided musings of others. In
fact, I had no room for them in my box of 'give a shit',
which was tucked neatly under the head of my bed the last
I checked – back in eighth grade.

Not particularly wanting to, I rolled over. My bed was a comfy place that felt as much like a cloud as anything man-made could – except, of course, those indoor, human-induced clouds used for existentialism and ogling about the power of Man versus God.

Falling to the floor, it must've groaned as much as I had. The floor was the exact opposite of my fluffy, loving bed. It was hardwood, unforgiving.

I got up and moved around my room. I could hear the cars drive along the street outside my window. I heard my mother and sisters drive each other insane through their every-morning ritual in the other direction, the direction of the hallway door. I chose neither and headed for my closet.

"You have a game today."

Spinning around, I caught sight of Abigail. I hadn't heard the door open but it must've. My littlest sister was sitting cross-legged innocently on the center of my bed. She wasn't innocent; her eyes glowed like the devil's did once he realized that the Lord allowed for earthquakes and tornados to be a part of His 'beautiful' creation.

"I know I have a game today. Get out of my room." I was lucky that I hadn't shucked my boxers away. She would have been met with a yelling and, probably, highly frustrated older brother which would only have added to her embarrassment; she really needed to learn how to knock.

She leaned back onto locked elbows and made a nonchalant look to the door. She flicked her legs out in front of her and crossed them at the ankles. She needed only a new pair of sunglasses and a beach to look like the front of a Target advertisement – and maybe a bathing suit instead of her Ariel pajamas. "My friends are coming to the game to sit with me."

A shudder flowed through me. It wasn't the good kind of shudder; it was the kind that one got when they felt like they were being followed. Her friends had an obsession with the school baseball team; a weird, obtusely stalkerish obsession. I had accidentally heard some of their late-Saturday-night truths that were said in the confidence of The Circle in the family room:

"Matt has a fabulous bottom when he wears his baseball tights."

"They're called knee-breeches."

"I don't care what they're actually called; we should call them butt-enhancers."

Giggles erupted.

"Speaking of good butts, Jared!"

Squealing commenced.

"I think Jared has the best arm muscles, too."

"Ooh, truth: Do you like Jared?"

There was a pause. "Maybe..."

Her confession was followed by another ripple of giggles.

Shaking away the thoughts of teenage girls, I returned to my original objective. "Will you leave my room so I can get ready for my 'fans'?"

She wrinkled her nose. "Are you talking about my friends or the other girls?"

I glared. I turned to my closet and removed my pressed uniform – complete with the grass-stain-less – not without a lot of work – 'butt-enhancers'. "The ones that wouldn't get me arrested to act upon their whims."

She shrugged, pulling another expression worthy of the devil onto her face – a smirk. "They'd all consent."

"Get out of my room!"

She hopped off my bed and moved out the door. "In two years, they'll all be old enough."

I smirked at her. "Yeah, but you've contaminated them all."

She tied her face into small cinched knots; her nose pinched and her lips pursed. She was in the hallway and had her head between the door and the doorframe. "Just the marinating you need, yeah?"

I threw clothes onto the bed and pulled my nightshirt off over my head. "I don't have the same palate as you. I like things... spicier." Which was definitely true. I'd taken to adding hot sauce to most All-American-baseball-arena delicacies while my youngest sister had courted ketchup since her stay in Hotel Mother-Dearest.

My sister closed the door just in time to enter a yelling match with the 'other' sister:

Lauren: "Abigail, this is your fault!"

Abigail: "What do you mean?"

Lauren: "I was taking a shower and the water turned cold."

Abigail: "So what; I wasn't in there but five minutes."

Lauren: "But you know how long my showers need to be; I have to look acceptable at the park!"

Abigail: "Whatever."

Doors slammed and one of my sisters – probably Abigail – stomped down the stairs; just the white noise of a typical morning.

I put the final touches on my uniform. The knee socks had to snap down over the laces and meet the bottom of the 'butt-enhancers' – what can I say, I kind of like the terminology – and the cap had to be at just the right angle for the pregame – the fashion show portion of the day.

Scene 2

I listened to ensure my safety to the kitchen. My sisters were like two tornados, one was small and speedy while the menacing other threatened to touch down at any moment.

Opening the door enough to peer out, I surveyed the hall. No signs of life: green light. I made my way through the minefield that doubled as the upstairs hallway to smile at my mom and dad. On my way, I placed my phone on the charging station by the hall closet. Our family had a rule:

You don't carry your phone on the first floor; the first floor is for talking and trying to be an actual family.

It didn't always work.

My mom manned the stove with all of her five-foot two-inch frame and my dad did the same with the newspaper at the same height only sitting – standing he was too tall to back talk. My mother jingled and jangles, decked out like a Christmas tree, only worse. She had on a 'Howlers Booster Club' mock-jersey, earrings, headband, knee socks identical to our guest game uniforms, and her shoelaces had been replaced by our team colors, orange and purple.

"How are you this morning?" She moved something in one of the four pans on the stove. Lauren was a vegetarian and had her own pan of separate everything. Abigail didn't like eggs so she had some grits going on the stove. There was a pan of scrambled eggs for the family – minus Abigail. Finally, the most important pan was the griddle pan with the hash browns and bacon for the sane people.

I wasn't entirely sure that I could count my mother as sane, though, based upon her gaudy ridiculousness she called her 'arena outfit'.

"Good." I removed my cap and sat at the table next to the paper. It wasn't really my dad until he put it down and it was revealed to be him. A small part of me, the juvenile part of me, liked to consider it like Schrödinger's Paradox: It both is and is not my dad, for all I know we have another person in the house who happens to enjoy the paper as much as my dad or, like most people, simply reads it because it is a sort of societal expectation; either way, not absolutely my dad.

I tried to ignore the paper but instead it spoke. "You ready for the game?"

It was the usual morning nothing-substantial. Maybe the stranger had a voice just like my dad? Still not truly my dad. It was a game of reality suspension; I played it often. My highest score is about two hours while I was sitting on the couch and refused to turn around and acknowledge that it was my dad at the dining room table.

I played with my hat on the table and wondered why my mother was taking too long to put the conversation-ender on the table. There is no excuse from conversation like shoving food into your mouth and blaming it on being a growing male. "I think we all are ready. We've practiced a lot for this one."

The paper crinkled a bit. It wasn't the sort of thing one could gauge a reaction from. I placed my cap over my finger and spun it around.

My mom put Lauren's vegetarian hash onto the table. "Lauren, come down to eat."

Lauren didn't come through the swing door. I wished she would. Maybe dad could fire some of his pointed normalcy at her. I wanted to not be the only offspring in the room.

"Abigail is to blame! I look hideous because she used all the water!"

The voice came from just above us, Lauren's room. I snickered. Lauren usually spent the games pretending that she was related to me and Abigail and not Mom or Dad. It made sense. Mom and Dad could be downright embarrassing.

"You probably look fine dear, come down here." Mom placed a plate in front of me, but still no food for face-shoving.

Abigail glided in. She slid around in her socks. She was on the school's figure skating team, but it was only a winter sport so she was done with Dad's expectations for the academic year. She had met all of them, of course, but she was still young and really – really – good at figure skating.

She slid to her seat after kissing the paper on the cheek. "Morning." She picked up her spoon to dig in but the food wasn't there. She shot me a horrified expression.

"Good morning, Abigail. Who are you meeting today?" The paper shifted.

She shot me a look for help. I shrugged. The paper, while it hid the enemy, made strategizing easier. I pointed to Mom who was moving her hips in time with the spoon in the grits.

Abigail sat back in her chair, calculating. "I'm meeting Jenna and Mary and Steph-... Stephanie."

I gave her a thumbs up, knowing that she changed 'Stephen' to 'Stephanie' to avoid the paper's hatred for boyfriends after Lauren's – many – failed attempts at courting.

The paper shifted again, but before it could reply, Lauren entered. We were the kind of offspring that occurred about eleven months of each other; twelfth, eleventh, and ninth grades each had their fair share of Dad's passive-aggressive teachers-don't-teach-right and Mom's you-are-the-best-teacher-ever attitudes.

"My hair is horrible." She turned to me. "Why do you have to be so popular? Would it kill you to be a nerd or something?"

"I am a nerd. I just happen to be on the baseball team, too." I shrugged and thanked the Lord in the Highest of Highs that my mother put food in front of me. I began to eat, keeping food in my mouth but also making sure it would last until something else was on my plate.

"Lauren, you look lovely." All three of the offspring glared at the paper wondering how it could say that if it had not seen her. It seemed to think we were oblivious to that fact but, obviously, we weren't.

My mother poured grits into Abigail's bowl. She darted to the fridge for cheese.

"Thanks, Dad." She replied, seeking closure to the discussion but not really believing it. Lauren flipped her hair over her shoulder. It was long and dark and shiny and I didn't think it looked particularly different than any other day.

The paper shifted.

A phone buzzed in the hallway on the charging station. We had no way of knowing whose it was and we weren't allowed to go check; it was a rule:

Phones don't interrupt meals.

I looked over with eggs half way to my mouth. Lauren glanced over forgetting that her hand was poised just behind her shoulder from where she had been playing with her hair. Abigail turned around in her chair holding both her bowl and her spoon.

Even my mom tilted a bit to the side to peek into the hallway.

The paper merely, minutely, shifted again.

Read More in

Spork

By Msknowitall

(It's from before I came out. I'll be
changing it over to MxKnowitall in the
near future.)